Michael Underwood and The Murder Room

>>> This title is part of The Murder Room, our series dedicated to making available out-of-print or hard-to-find titles by classic crime writers.

Crime fiction has always held up a mirror to society. The Victorians were fascinated by sensational murder and the emerging science of detection; now we are obsessed with the forensic detail of violent death. And no other genre has so captivated and enthralled readers.

Vast troves of classic crime writing have for a long time been unavailable to all but the most dedicated frequenters of second-hand bookshops. The advent of digital publishing means that we are now able to bring you the backlists of a huge range of titles by classic and contemporary crime writers, some of which have been out of print for decades.

From the genteel amateur private eyes of the Golden Age and the femmes fatales of pulp fiction, to the morally ambiguous hard-boiled detectives of mid twentieth-century America and their descendants who walk our twenty-first century streets, The Murder Room has it all. >>>

The Murder Room
Where Criminal Minds Meet

themurderroom.com

Michael Underwood (1916–1992)

Michael Underwood (the pseudonym of John Michael Evelyn) was born in Worthing, Sussex and educated at Christ Church College, Oxford. He was called to the Bar in 1939 and served in the British army during World War Two. He returned to work in the Department of Public Prosecutions until his retirement in 1976, and wrote almost 50 crime novels informed by his career in the law. His five series characters include Sergeant Nick Atwell and lawyer Rosa Epton, of whom is was said by the *Washington Post* that she 'outdoes Perry Mason'.

Rosa Epton
A Pinch of Snuff
Crime upon Crime
Double Jeopardy
Goddess of Death
A Party to Murder
Death in Camera
The Hidden Man
Death at Deepwood Grange
The Injudicious Judge
The Uninvited Corpse
Dual Enigma
A Compelling Case
A Dangerous Business
Rosa's Dilemma
The Seeds of Murder
Guilty Conscience

Murder with Malice
Crooked Wood

Standalone titles
A Crime Apart
Shem's Demise
The Silent Liars
Anything But the Truth
Smooth Justice
Victim of Circumstance
A Clear Case of Suicide
The Hand of Fate

A Pinch of Snuff

Michael Underwood

An Orion book

Copyright © Isobel Mackenzie 1974

The right of Michael Underwood to be identified as the author of this work has been asserted in accordance with the Copyright, Designs and Patents Act 1988.

This edition published by
The Orion Publishing Group Ltd
Orion House
5 Upper St Martin's Lane
London WC2H 9EA

An Hachette UK company
A CIP catalogue record for this book is available from the British Library

ISBN 978 1 4719 0457 8

www.orionbooks.co.uk

CHAPTER ONE

Compared with the rest of life, the Blackstone Club had, during its one hundred and ninety years of existence, been scarcely touched by time. Indeed, it had become a cliché for guests to comment, as they gazed at the heavy furnishings and the seeming tiers of portraits of unremarkable Georgian judges and sternly complacent Victorian ones, that they felt as if they had stepped back a century.

Sometimes, of course, a carpet had to be replaced or one of the huge black leather armchairs in the smoking-room was sent away for repair, but the work was always so artfully accomplished that nothing ever had the impudence to give an impression of newness.

It might truthfully be said that the only aspect of the club to suffer change at all was the membership itself. Inevitably death took its toll, but, as members were drawn exclusively from the legal profession—and the more senior reaches at that—an air of sameness was perpetuated, lawyers not being noted for innovation of appearance.

Ex-Judge Whitby-Stansford, who had not grown mellower with the years, threw down *The Times* with an impatient gesture and glared at the baroque marble clock which stood above the fireplace. From the clock his gaze went to the bell-push and from that, hopefully, to the occupant of the chair opposite him.

Hugh Eversley Q.C. was not only considerably younger

than the retired judge, but he was also closer to the bell. Unfortunately, he appeared buried in the magazine he was reading and remained undistracted by the small pantomime that was going on opposite him. At length, ex-Judge Whitby-Stansford was forced into speech.

'Mind giving the bell a push for me?'

'Certainly.' Eversley put his magazine down and leaned over to reach the bell. 'If it's working.'

Apparently it was and half a minute later the smoking-room door opened and a long-haired young man wearing a blue linen jacket entered.

'Bring me a large pink gin,' ex-Judge Whitby-Stansford said a trifle breathlessly as he struggled to pick *The Times* up from the floor.

'Anything for you, sir?' the young wine steward said, looking at Eversley.

'No, thank you.'

'What's that young man's name?' the ex-judge asked after he had left.

'I think it's Brian.'

'Brian's his surname, I take it?'

'I imagine it's his first name.'

'Since when have the Blackstone's male servants been known by their Christian names?'

Hugh Eversley gave a faint shrug and smiled. 'He seems a very obliging youth for all that. It's not easy to get young staff these days. Not much money and Talbot can be a bit of a tyrant to these young men.'

'Damn good club servant, Talbot. Been here over forty years. Trouble is, the young these days don't know what service means.' He gave the rumpled *Times* a menacing shake. 'Have you read that letter in here by that left-wing M.P. chap running down British justice?' Eversley nodded warily, as ex-Judge Whitby-Stansford went on in a belligerent tone, 'Seems to be all the fashion nowadays, denigrating your country's proudest institutions. Don't know why he doesn't go and live in Russia if he really feels the way he pretends he does. He'd then learn quickly enough that British justice is second to none. It's our greatest bulwark against these left-wing dictator types.' He gave *The Times* a further angry shake. 'It's their intellectual arrogance that gets my goat. I don't mind telling you, Eversley, that despite the rising crime rate and all these long-haired layabouts you see around everywhere, I wouldn't want to see our jury system changed for any other. May sound odd coming from an old reactionary like myself, but I believe in the old adage that it's better nine guilty men should go free than one innocent man should be wrongly convicted.'

'I agree,' Eversley said with a nod and moved to pick up his magazine, but ex-Judge Whitby-Stansford hadn't yet finished.

'Once that concept goes by the board, justice in this country will be on the slippery slope.' He put out a hand and took the glass with which the wine steward had just returned to the room. 'I have great faith in the good sense of the British juror,' he added energetically, taking a gulp of pink gin.

The wine steward, whose name was Brian Tanner, couldn't help grinning to himself as he made his way out of the smoking-room. After all, nobody had reason to feel better disposed towards British justice than he. On two occasions in his short life, he had faced trial and on each, though as guilty as hell, had been acquitted, thanks to benevolent juries.

Silence fell again in the smoking-room after Brian had left. Hugh Eversley returned successfully to the magazine he'd been reading and ex-Judge Whitby-Stansford ambled across to the table on which various books of reference were kept and went into a huddle with a copy of *Who's Who*. About five minutes later, he made to leave the room.

'You dining here tonight by any chance?' he enquired, as he reached the door.

'No. I'm only killing time before I go and meet my wife,' Eversley replied. 'We're going to Covent Garden.'

'Don't envy you. There's only one thing worse than opera and that's ballet.'

'You're not alone in that view,' Eversley said with a smile.

'Suppose you're not going to that sale of Georgian silver at Christies next week?'

'No. I'm afraid I know next to nothing about old silver. Incidentally, I gather the club has been presented with another snuff-box for its collection.'

Ex-Judge Whitby-Stansford let out a small snort. 'Early Victorian. Plain mother of pearl with a silver mount. Neither attractive nor particularly valuable. Don't know why we accepted it. Told the committee so, too.' With this parting shot, he disappeared through the door.

It so happened that Brian was standing near the glass-topped cases in which the club's collection of snuff-boxes was kept when the ex-judge crossed the inner hall. He moved discreetly to one side as the old man veered towards the cases and paused to gaze at them, his expression one of greedy absorption.

Brian couldn't help noticing that one particular item seemed to hold the ex-judge's attention and, after he had moved on his way again, he walked over to the cases to see which it had been. It looked as if it might have been an ornate gold one which had pride of place in the centre of the particular case.

Brian cast an idle eye over the whole collection before returning to the wine steward's pantry to await his next summons. He knew they were worth a tidy fortune and they were certainly nice to look at, but there was no point in *his* getting ideas about them. They were outside his class and, anyway, he was under different instructions.

When he reached the pantry, Talbot was fussing with a tray of drinks.

'I'm serving Sir John and his guests,' he said importantly. 'He has Lord Crayford and Sir Douglas to dinner.'

Brian gave him a bemused look. He knew Sir John must be the Honourable Sir John Pearn, chairman of the Blackstone Club and a High Court judge. He neither knew, nor cared, who were Lord Crayford or Sir Douglas.

'Want a hand?' he enquired helpfully.

'No, but just hand me that cloth. Whoever dried this glass must have used a dirty rag! I don't know what Sir John's guests would think!'

Brian watched him impassively as he polished the offending glass and held it up to the light. Then picking up the tray with the drinks set out on it, he made to leave the pantry.

'By the way, Brian, somebody tried to phone you a short while ago,' he said as he steered himself through the door.

'Me?' Brian asked in surprise.

'It was a man. Said he wanted to speak to Brian Tanner and that's you, isn't it?' Talbot's tone was waspish as it was inclined to become when dealing with junior staff. 'Wouldn't leave a message. Said he'd call again later.'

After Talbot had gone, Brian stood staring at the rows of bottles which lined one wall. Only one person knew he was working at the Blackstone and that was Fiona. And she had never called him there and, anyway, she wasn't a man.

Brian was puzzled.

CHAPTER TWO

The Blackstone Club was tucked away between the back of the Law Courts and Lincoln's Inn Fields, much closer to the law's own precincts than the Garrick, which had a quota of legal members but was not exclusively legal. There was nothing to please the eye about its façade which was grey and plain and seemed to have acquired a pinched, resentful air with the encroachment of a number of modern multi-storey buildings.

Brian came off duty at eight o'clock that evening and was off the premises by one minute past. He walked quickly up to Holborn underground station and caught a train to Baron's Court. From there it was a ten minutes walk to the room off the North End Road which he shared with Fiona.

It was a tall Victorian house, owned by an Indian and let off in rooms which the owner was pleased to call flats. Flat eight was Fiona's and Brian had moved in not long after meeting her a few months before. Quite often other people, friends of Fiona's, would spend the night there, too. While she and Brian occupied the bed, it was nothing to have one or two of either sex and any colour stretched out on the floor. Brian didn't much care for this arrangement and Fiona would tease him about being a working-class puritan.

But on the whole it was a satisfactory association which suited Brian for the time being (it wasn't his nature to plan ahead, in any event) and which also obviously pleased Fiona.

When he reached the door of their flat, he could see a light shining beneath and so knocked rather than fiddle with his own key.

'Hello, love,' Fiona said stepping aside to let him enter and then clasping his head in both her hands and giving him a smacking kiss. She was wearing an ankle-length coat of coarse, shaggy hair that made her resemble a slim yak. Her head was swathed in a bright orange bandeau. She kissed him a second time. 'I'm just going out, love. I'll be back around eleven.'

'Where are you going?'

'One of our meetings,' she said casually. 'What'll you do?'

He shrugged. 'You didn't phone me at the club this evening, did you?'

'No, love.'

'Someone did.'

She looked at him sharply. 'You sound worried.'

'Not really worried. Puzzled. I can't think who it could have been. You're the only person who knows I'm working there. Well, you and some of your friends.'

'It's certainly not in any of their interests to open their mouths.'

'Then somebody must have recognised me.'

'But that was all checked very carefully. None of the barristers connected with either of your cases, nor the judges, are members of the Blackstone Club.' Her expression cleared. 'Anyway, what are we fussing about when you don't even know who the caller was or why he wanted to speak to you. The whole thing could easily be a mistake. A wrong number, a wrong identity, something of that sort. I must leave you, love,' she said hurriedly. She kissed him again, picked up her lighter and a packet of cigarettes from the bed and shot through the door.

The room felt curiously empty after her departure. It

always did and Brian supposed this was part of her attraction though he never bothered to analyse his feelings. On her part, together with all the vitality and energetic pursuit of causes, there was a maternalism which found expression in her genuine care for Brian. She was not only two years older than him (twenty-five to his twenty-three), but a far more dominating character. Not to mention a much better educated one, though each would have denied that this had any relevance to their relationship.

After spending half an hour trying to make up his mind what to do, he went out to the nearest pub. Two pints of beer later, he returned to the flat and went to bed.

He didn't hear Fiona come back and the next morning she was still asleep when he got up to go to work.

He had just taken a pre-lunch gin and tonic to Arnold Feely, who was probably the club's most sartorially elegant member—and certainly one of its youngest—and returned to the wine steward's pantry when one of the kitchen staff stuck his head round the door and told him he was wanted on the phone.

'That Brian Tanner?' a voice enquired when he picked up the receiver. It was a voice with a strong cockney accent.

'Yes, who's that speaking?' Brian's own voice indicated his nervousness.

'I think I can do you a good turn, Brian,' the voice went on shifting into a warmer tone. 'Can we meet when you finish work this evening and I'll tell you what I 'ave in mind.'

'What sort of a good turn?'

'A financial one. What time do you get off?'

'I'm off at five today.'

'That's fine. I'll meet you at half past five in the lobby of the Strand Palace Hotel. Don't be late because I know you're going to be glad you came.'

At that moment, Talbot loomed in the niche where the staff telephone was situated.

'I do wish you'd tell your friends not to phone you just before lunch,' he said petulantly. 'I can't serve everyone on my own. Now get along to the smoking-room. They've rung twice already.'

Brian hurried off to do as he was bidden, glad to have his mind distracted by work. Nevertheless, the afternoon wore by very slowly and he found himself looking at his watch almost every five minutes.

For once, he was on time for an appointment. Indeed, it was a few minutes before the half-hour when he entered the hotel lobby. Nobody took any notice of him as he glanced shyly about him. He had not advanced very far and was wondering whereabouts he had better stand when a familiar voice spoke at his side.

'Brian Tanner?'

He turned his head to find a small man with thinning hair looking at him.

'Yes.'

'I thought it must be you,' said the man. 'Let's get out of this crowd and find somewhere quiet where we can talk. There's a café round the back.'

He headed for the door and Brian followed. Though he had a slightly down-at-heel appearance—his brown suit had not only seen better days but been cut for a larger frame than that on which it now hung—he moved nimbly and with confidence. He had a narrow head and his rather elongated ears lay flat so that the general appearance was of his head having been caught in a press.

A few minutes later they entered an almost empty café. Brian's companion nodded to the man who presided behind the counter and led the way to a table at the back.

'Two teas and two cheese rolls,' he called out when they were seated.

'Now I expect you're wondering what this is all about,'

he said after they had been served. 'First of all, let me introduce myself. I'm 'Arry. 'Arry Green. And as I told you on the phone, I'm in line to do you a good turn.' He rubbed the fingers and thumb of his right hand together. 'Money, that's what we all need, isn't it? The more the better. And the easier it's earned the better still. That's what I'm going to do for you, Brian, help you earn some easy money. What do you say to that?'

'I'll tell you when I've heard more.'

'Good lad, Brian. That's what I like, a bit of caution at the right time. You're a man after my own 'eart. 'Arry Green never got bounced into anything, I'll tell you that now.' His glance which had darted like a lizard's tongue suddenly settled on Brian's face. 'I think you and me already understand each other pretty well, Brian.' He grinned knowingly, revealing long, stained teeth which guarded his mouth like a weathered stockade. 'Do you know why you agreed to meet me, Brian? Shall I tell you?' Brian nodded. 'It wasn't just because you were interested in what I said. After all, I could 'ave been setting you a trap.' He leaned forward and, emphasising his words with a bony finger, went on, 'You came, Brian, not just out of interest. Getting you interested was the easy part. The difficult part was to persuade you to overcome your natural suspicion about what might be in store for you. That's where the psychological approach came in, Brian. You came because I suggested a nice, innocent place to meet. The lobby of a big, crowded 'otel. Nothing nasty could 'appen to you there. Am I right, Brian? Am I right?' He paused to take a bite of his cheese roll and then continued as if Brian's assent could be taken for granted. 'And you've noticed that from the moment we met, I've taken charge? That's also the psychological approach. 'Ad to impress you! Even ordered you a cheese roll without asking first.' He cast an eye on Brian's untouched roll. 'If you don't want yours, I'll 'ave it. But now we already understand each other,' he added, after Brian had pushed his plate towards him. There was a moment's silence while Harry Green filled his mouth with cheese roll and tea, then he went on, 'And since we understand each other, it's time to come to the point. Agree, Brian?'

'Agree.'

'The subject for discussion is snuff-boxes, removal of.'

Brian started and Harry Green gave him an amused look.

'Surprised, are you? Not what you expected, eh?'

'Go on.'

'The Blackstone Club has one of the finest collections of snuff-boxes outside of a museum,' Harry Green intoned as if he were an official guide. 'They're valued at twenty-five thousand pounds and they could probably fetch quite a bit more than that if they were 'andled in the right way.'

'If you think I'm going to risk my neck...'

Harry Green held up an admonitory hand. 'Wait a moment, Brian lad! You 'aven't 'eard it all yet, 'ave you? Not like you to jump in before you know what's coming. Remember, you and I understand each other. O.K.?' Brian gave a reluctant nod. 'I mean if you don't want to 'ear the rest, all you've got to do is just get up and walk out and you'll never see me again. On the other 'and, I don't think that's what you do want and it's not a course of action I'd advise, because then you'd be doing yourself a bad turn. O.K.? Shall I go on now?'

'Yes, go on,' Brian said evenly.

'Now the great thing about snuff-boxes is that they're small. You could almost carry thousands of pounds worth of 'em away in your pockets without their showing.'

'The ones at the Blackstone are under heavy lock and key.'

Harry Green gave him a pained look. 'Who's telling who, Brian? Of course, they're under lock and key. One set of keys is held by the secretary, the other set is kept in his office by day and, at night, is taken up to bed by old Talbot. As you know 'e's the only person who sleeps on the premises.'

Brian said nothing. There was nothing he felt he could say. It was obvious that Harry Green knew a great deal about the Blackstone's property, not to mention the club's internal arrangements. Green went on:

'Enough said, I think, to show you this is a serious proposition. Stage two will be to tell you the part you'll be expected to play in the painless removal of those little old snuff-boxes.' He gave Brian a sly look and said, 'But perhaps first I should tell you what's in it for Brian Tanner. That's what you want to hear most, isn't it, Brian lad? And let me be the first to say, what's more natural! FIVE HUNDRED QUID, that's what's in it for you. Yes, five hundred of the best. And all for less than an hour's work.' He chuckled. 'I can see from the light in your eyes that you're interested. And so you should be, it's not often you can earn that sort of money so easy.'

'What am I expected to do? Mind you, I'm not saying I will, but you can't expect me to agree to something before I know what it is.'

'That's right, Brian. We're understanding each other again.' Harry Green thrust a hand across the table. 'It's time to shake on it,' he said solemnly. Feeling faintly embarrassed, Brian put out his own hand, wondering, as he did so, if this was another aspect of his companion's psychological approach.

'Now here's the plan,' Green went on. 'We choose an evening when you come off duty at half past eight. Then just before the club closes at eleven thirty and old Talbot locks up, you slip back inside and 'ide. You know he takes a glass of 'ot milk up to bed with 'im? And I expect you know he always washes down 'is sleeping pill with it. Well, on this particular evening when 'e's on 'is final rounds

12

with 'is glass of 'ot milk all ready to take upstairs, 'e'll get a phone call. One of the members' wives thinks she must 'ave left 'er bag in the visitors' dining-room. Will Talbot kindly go and see. 'E puts down 'is milk and goes off. While 'e's away, you pop a sleeping pill into 'is milk. It'll be a good strong one to ensure that 'e goes off into the land of nod in record time. With me?'

Brian nodded in rapt attention.

'When 'e's asleep, you'll slip up to 'is room and get 'old of the keys which 'e always puts on the bedside table. You come downstairs, unlock the door at the back, where yours truly will be waiting, then you unlock the cases where the little old snuff-boxes are kept. When it's all over, you lock up everywhere again, put the keys back in Talbot's room and find somewhere to 'ave a bit of kip yourself. Then the next morning after the old sod has come down and un-locked the back door, you take the opportunity of slip-ping out without anyone ever knowing you've spent the night there. As far as the rest of the world is concerned, you went off duty at eight thirty the previous evening and don't return to the club until after the bit of old grand larceny has been discovered.' Green paused. 'Neat, isn't it? Nothing overlooked. A real gem of a little scheme. Now you can believe me when I said I wanted to do you a good turn. It'll be the quickest and easiest five hundred quid you'll ever earn, Brian lad.'

When he finished speaking, Harry Green picked up the remains of Brian's cheese roll and stuffed it into his mouth. It was as if he had decided to give Brian a few quiet moments to mull things over, for he suddenly rose and went across to the counter to order another cup of tea. When he returned, he said cheerfully, 'Well, 'ow does it appeal to you, Brian?'

Brian shrugged indifferently. 'Can't say until you tell me the rest.'

'What do you mean?'

'Somebody's worked out a neat scheme all right. Who is it? It certainly isn't you.'

A nasty look came into Harry Green's eyes. 'It doesn't matter who it is. You're being offered five 'undred quid on a plate. You're daft if you don't take it. You're worse than daft because I don't think they'll take no for an answer.'

'Who's they?'

'What's it matter? I thought you were a pro. Pros don't ask silly questions.'

'Who put you on to me?'

'Questions, questions,' Green said in an exasperated voice. 'Look, Brian, I'll come clean with you. My instructions were to contact you and get your co-operation. I'm not saying who gave me my instructions but 'e's not the big guy anyway. There are others beyond him whose names I don't know. What's more I don't want to know. The less you sometimes know, the better. All I'm doing is selling a service, but I need an assistant and you're the bloke who's been chosen.'

Brian licked his lips slowly. 'And if I refuse?'

'Christ! I thought we'd been through all that. If you refuse, I merely report the fact. What 'appens after that is nothing to do with me.' He gave Brian a hard look through narrowed eyes. 'Well?'

Brian whose mind had been revving all the time like a jet before take-off decided the moment had come to declare himself.

'If I do it, I'll want more than five hundred,' he said baldly.

Green's breath came out in a whistle as if he had just been poked in the kidneys.

''Ow much more?' he asked.

'I reckon a thousand would be nearer the mark. You can't manage without me and I ought to receive proper payment for the job.'

'Proper little trade unionist, aren't you!'

'It's up to you.'

'I'll 'ave to talk to my boss, but 'e's not going to like it, not one little bit.'

'Someone obviously miscalculated in thinking he could get me cheap,' Brian said, with a faint smile. 'I also have a service to sell.'

'Don't blame me if you get your tail twisted bad, Brian lad. I'll put to them what you've said and let you know.'

'I reckon I can look after myself all right,' Brian replied.

'I hope you can,' Harry Green said nastily, 'but I wonder if you know which league you're trying to play in.' He rose and buttoned the ill-fitting jacket of his suit. 'What time'll you be at the Blackstone Club tomorrow?'

'Ten o'clock.'

'Stand by for a call from me at 'alf past.'

A second later he had gone, leaving Brian staring at the remnants of their exiguous meal. He remained deep in thought for several minutes. He had, after all, been given enough food for thought to last him several days.

Four things stuck out in his mind as a result of the meeting with Harry Green. He was tempted to fall in with the plan even if he couldn't screw more money out of them. Five hundred quid wasn't bad for a few hours' work, though there'd been no reason not to try and get a bit more. Secondly, there were the veiled threats if he didn't agree to co-operate. These might only be so much bluff, but one couldn't know for sure and the fact that there were clearly bigger figures in the background gave them some substance. Next, there was the undoubted fact that someone had been expertly primed as to the club's nightly routine at closing time. Lastly—and this is what bothered Brian's mind most of all—someone must know about *him*.

His most recent acquittal had been at the Old Bailey four months before and he had been working at the Blackstone Club for just under two months. He had spent a week or so in custody when first arrested on the charge of stealing a cheque book from one of the customers of the night-club where he had been temporarily employed as a waiter—the job had been more temporary than he'd intended—but none of those he'd briefly rubbed shoulders with in Brixton prison could have known he was working at the Blackstone. And before he started there, not only had Fiona assured him that none of the lawyers he'd had anything to do with were members, but he had subsequently confirmed this by checking the club list. Moreover, he hadn't seen anyone on the premises whom he faintly recognised; and he had a good memory for faces.

All he could conclude was that one of Fiona's lot—he always thought of them as a 'lot'—must have talked out of turn, whatever she might say. They seemed to have mysterious contacts everywhere, so it could well have come about. Brian had no illusions about the number of effective grapevines in operation amongst those who lived part, if not all, of their lives outside the law.

But it was an accomplished fact. Someone knew of his proclivities and also knew that he was working at the Blackstone Club. That made him an obvious choice of inside man in the planned theft of the snuff-boxes. His feeling of unease remained unresolved, but was it a reason for refusing to co-operate? He decided that it quite definitely wasn't. Indeed, if he agreed to join in, not only would he be a thousand pounds richer—well, five hundred, at any rate—but he also stood a better chance of finding out how he had come to be propositioned.

He rose from the table and made his way out of the café, collecting a hard, suspicious look, as he passed, from the man behind the counter.

CHAPTER THREE

Harry Green's call came through exactly on time the next morning. Brian, who had been hovering near the staff phone, leapt at it at the first ring.

Green accepted his assent without comment. There was no indication of relief, let alone of enthusiasm. There was also no mention of money, though Brian was instructed to meet him in the same café again that evening.

The rest of the day seemed a bit of an anti-climax. There were fewer members than usual in for lunch and the afternoon was always a dead period. Those members who were still active returned to work, leaving a few like ex-Judge Whitby-Stansford to fill the smoking-room with the sound of heavy breathing and muted snores until it was time to order their pots of tea and buttered toast.

Brian was on duty until seven this particular evening. At six o'clock he was instructed by Talbot to go up to the 'snuff-room' where there was a meeting of the 'bequests' sub-committee and to take their order for drinks. He was normally punctilious about serving the various sub-committees himself, as well as the full committee when it met, but his rheumatism was bothering him ('my screws are bad today,' he had earlier told Brian) and so he had reluctantly surrendered the duty to his junior.

'Don't forget, you first ask Sir John what he'd like and then the other members.'

'I thought Sir John always had the same. That Tio Pepe sherry.'

'Good gracious,' Talbot exclaimed, his tone scandalised.

'You'll next be handing him the bottle and telling him to pour it himself. Anyway, he might suddenly decide to have something different. Now, are you clear what you do?'

'Yes. Ask them in turn what they want, starting with Sir John.'

'Off you go then.'

The snuff-room was on a floor of its own, about half a dozen steps up from the first floor landing. It was a convenient room for committee meetings and private gatherings, but was otherwise seldom used.

The sound of laughter greeted Brian's ears as he arrived outside the door. He knocked and went in. Sir John Pearn sat at the head of the table, with Colonel Tatham the club secretary on his right. Next to the secretary was Arnold Feely. Opposite these two were Robert Stacey, a Chancery silk, and Philip Maxwell, who was a High Court registrar.

'Ah!' said Sir John as he turned to see Brian in the doorway. 'Talbot has lifted the siege. I'm going to have a Tio Pepe. What about everyone else?'

One by one they gave their orders as Brian stood there with an obliging smile on his face.

'Can you really remember that lot?' Sir John enquired in a friendly voice.

'Yes, sir. One Tio Pepe. Two gin and tonics. A gin and french with ice and a glass of champagne.'

'Good for you. It's more than I could.' Brian retired to an accompaniment of warm smiles and, turning to the secretary, Sir John said, 'Seems rather a good lad, Tatham. Both efficient and obliging, which, as we know from experience, don't necessarily come together.'

The secretary, a morose man who had never really come to terms with his retirement job as a club secretary, nodded but added gloomily, 'Trouble is if they're any good, they don't stay. Heaven knows what'll happen when Talbot goes.'

'The club seems to have managed pretty well for a hundred and ninety years,' Sir John said in a dry tone, 'and Talbot's only been here for the last forty of them.' He glanced round to reap approving smiles from everyone save Colonel Tatham. 'Anyway, where were we? Ah, yes, the matter of Miss Beresford's bequest. I take it that, despite Whitby-Stansford's demurrer, we are minded to confirm our acceptance of the offer as graciously as the offer itself was made? It belonged to her brother who died last year and who'd been, as you know, a member of the club for a quarter of a century. Apparently it was something he greatly prized—*pace* Whitby-Stansford—and it had been in the family for over a century. I seem to remember Miss Beresford said in her letter that it had originally belonged to their grandfather. It may not be as valuable as some of our others, but'—Sir John's tone became frostily judicial—'I trust the Blackstone has not yet sunk to judging everything by its insurance value.'

'To be fair to Whitby-Stansford,' Maxwell said, 'I don't think his objections were based entirely on its lack of value.'

'Probably not,' Sir John observed. 'He has, of course, a very fine collection of *objets d'art* himself and he's extremely knowledgeable on antiques generally. I accept—I'm sure we all accept—that his objection was founded solely on aesthetic grounds. Anyone got anything to add?'

'Just that it may be more valuable than we're led to believe,' Arnold Feely said with a diffidence that became the youngest and most junior person present. 'My wife was looking it up in one of her books of reference last night—I had mentioned it to her—and it seems a similar one was sold at Christies last year for two hundred pounds.'

'Whitby-Stansford would still consider that cheap, I imagine,' Sir John said with a sniff. He always found it difficult not to snub Feely. He recognised him as an effective advocate, though he was inclined to identify himself too vigorously with his client's cause. In court, he could be ingratiating one moment and show brash indifference to the bench the next. Sir John was personally regretful when he was elected a member of the Blackstone, but his candidature was well supported and there was nothing now to be done about that, anyway.

If Feely felt reproved, he certainly didn't show it. On his part, he regarded Sir John as someone who had to be lived with, in and out of court.

On his way back upstairs to the snuff-room with his tray of drinks, Brian noticed ex-Judge Whitby-Stansford bent over one of the display cases. His spectacles were up on his forehead and his face was almost pressed against the glass. Brian couldn't help smirking at the sudden thought of the old judge being the master-mind of a criminal organisation. As it was, the poor old sod wasn't even of any interest to Fiona's lot!

As soon as he came off duty, Brian hurried away to the café behind the Strand. Harry Green was already there, sitting at the same table they had occupied the previous evening.

'Fetch yourself a tea if you want one,' he said as Brian approached.

Brian paused by the counter while the proprietor poured a cup from an enormous teapot and slopped in some milk.

'It's fixed then for the day after tomorrow,' Green said when Brian had joined him at the table. 'No need to go through all the arrangements again.' He put his hand in his pocket and withdrew a small screw of paper. 'That's the pill to put into Talbot's milk. Anything else you want to know?' His tone was challenging and his voice had none of the artificial bonhomie of their previous meeting.

Brian was not prepared to be browbeaten, however. 'What about the money?' he asked.

'I warned you they weren't going to like it and they didn't. 'Owever, they've agreed to split the difference. It's seven fifty. And I don't mind telling you, you're a lucky lad. It's as well you weren't around when I reported your attitude or you mightn't be sitting in this snug little café now.'

'O.K., I'll do it for seven fifty,' Brian said, trying not to show the small sense of triumph he felt. 'When do I get it?'

Green stared at him as if he was holding out a begging bowl. 'You want to watch out, lad, that you don't trip over your greed and have a nasty fall.'

'When do I get it?' Brian repeated stolidly.

'I'm to give you a hundred on account, but just remember there's no turning back once your itchy little fingers 'ave touched it. You got that?'

'Who said anything about turning back?'

'I'm just reminding you, that's all.' He reached into the wallet pocket of his jacket and pulled out a crumpled envelope. 'It's in fivers. Twenty of 'em in there. Don't try and count 'em here. Just stick it in your pocket.'

Brian took the envelope and gave the contents a quick look before thrusting it into his hip pocket. The envelope certainly contained £5 notes and he didn't imagine they'd short-change him at this stage.

'And the remainder?' he enquired.

'I'm to give it to you as soon as the job's been completed.'

'You mean, before you leave the club?'

Green nodded. 'As I step through the door with the little old snuff-boxes, I 'and you the rest of the money. Satisfied at last?'

'Seems O.K.'

'Seems O.K.!' Green repeated with a sneer. 'That's the trouble of working with amateurs,' he added in a scornful mutter. He seemed about to make a further comment, but to check himself. 'The night after tomorrow, then—and no slip-ups.'

He rose quickly to his feet and walked from the café with the same nimble movements that contrasted so oddly with the rest of his appearance.

On this occasion, Brian didn't linger either, but hurried out under the surly gaze of the proprietor. But Harry Green was already lost to sight by the time he reached the pavement.

Fiona was lying on the bed when Brian got back to their room.

'Hello, love,' she said listlessly, 'I'm depressed.' She put out a hand and pulled him down beside her.

'Why are you depressed?' he enquired without great interest.

'It's just one of my black days. We all seem to be squabbling and getting nowhere and I sometimes wonder...' She shot up suddenly into a sitting position. 'That's defeatist talk! I don't wonder at all! I know we're right!' She turned her head and gave Brian a broad smile. 'And you, love, you're helping us. Doesn't that make you also feel terrific?'

Brian grinned. He didn't have much sympathy with their hare-brained ideas, but he had learnt that it was better not to say so to Fiona who was liable to launch a diatribe at him. As to help, he couldn't really believe he was much of that either, though it pleased Fiona to make out that he was an important element in the plans which she and her lot were busy hatching. At all events, it was certainly due to her that he'd taken the job at the Blackstone Club.

'I've just come from meeting Harry Green again,' he said, after a pause.

'Harry Green?' she said, vaguely.

'The chap who's going to nick the Blackstone's snuffboxes.'

'Oh, yes, him.'

'It's all fixed for the night after tomorrow.'

Her expression became worried. 'Are you sure it's safe, love? Safe for you, that is?'

'I reckon it's a good deal. I'm getting seven fifty quid,' he said with a note of pride.

'Then you'll be my stinking capitalist friend!' she said, giving him a kiss. 'I ought really to disown you. If the others knew...'

'You haven't told them?' he broke in, anxiously.

'Of course not!'

'You mustn't. If you did, I could really get put away.'

'I haven't told a soul and I shan't tell a soul.'

'The fact remains that somebody learnt about my working at the Blackstone.'

'I said this to Arthur and Hive and Roscoe, but they each swear they've never mentioned it outside our own walls.'

'But you haven't told them about the snuff-box business?'

With a dramatic gesture, Fiona placed a hand over her heart. 'I swear I haven't. I love you too much. Much more than you love me, in fact,' she added, reproachfully.

Brian sighed. Fiona's moods not only exhausted her, but could drain him as well if he allowed them. Love was her word, not his. He certainly liked her, was flattered by her attention except when she became too emotional, and he enjoyed the sex side of their relationship, except here again he sometimes found her too demanding.

'Will you do something for me, love?' she asked eagerly with another sudden twist of mood. 'Will you bring *me* a snuff-box?'

He looked at her in surprise. 'What for? And, anyway, it may be impossible.'

'Just one little snuff-box,' she said in a wheedling tone. 'The least valuable one in the collection will do. Please, love! I've suddenly got a wonderful idea, you see!'

CHAPTER FOUR

The next day saw an unanticipated encounter between the chairman of the Blackstone Club and Arnold Feely. Mr Justice Pearn was sitting at the Old Bailey and the case he was trying had to be abruptly adjourned when the accused became suddenly ill. This was in the early afternoon and he was then asked if he would deal with one transferred from another court which was a guaranteed plea of guilty and wouldn't last above half an hour.

'Who's defending?' he enquired.

'Feely,' said the clerk of the court.

'And you say it's a plea?' the judge remarked in some surprise.

'Feely has told me so himself.'

'Unusual for one of his clients to plead guilty. They generally fight all the way, making indiscriminate attacks on the police.'

A quarter of an hour later when they were all assembled in court, Arnold Feely's client duly pleaded guilty to three counts of indecently assaulting girls as they were walking home late at night. Prosecuting counsel outlined the facts from which it appeared to be one of the nastier cases of its sort. Though none of the girls had suffered any great physical harm, each had undergone an alarming experience. Eventually a trap had been set and the accused had been caught 'red-handed' as prosecuting counsel somewhat ambiguously put it. Apart from the last occasion, there was really not much evidence against Feely's client, but, nevertheless, he had chosen to plead guilty to all three charges.

On conclusion of his address, prosecuting counsel called into the witness-box Detective Sergeant Craddock who was the officer in charge of the case.

After he had taken the oath, Sergeant Craddock produced copies of the accused's antecedent history which he had prepared. These showed that the accused was forty-two years old and had been in prison on a number of previous occasions for a variety of offences including indecent assault.

'Yes, Mr Feely,' the judge said, when prosecuting counsel resumed his seat, 'I take it you wish to ask the officer some questions.'

'If your lordship pleases.' He turned towards the police officer, who was looking at him with a mixture of suspicion and hostility. Mr Justice Pearn had observed that most police officers wore such an expression when Feely rose to question them. 'Would I be right in saying, Sergeant Craddock,' Feely began in the friendliest of tones, 'that you have come to know the accused quite well in the course of your investigation?'

'Yes, sir, I think that's true.'

'And what sort of an impression has he made on you?'

'In respect of these offences, you mean?'

'Yes.'

'I think he's filled with remorse for what he's done.'

'That would appear to be borne out by his plea of guilty,' Feely said, giving the judge a meaning glance.

'I agree, sir.'

'Do you think that, if given the opportunity, he would benefit from treatment?'

'That's not for me to say, sir, but I accept that he's genuine in his desire to receive help of some sort.'

'Does he strike you as someone who has coped with his

faults to the best of his ability and who has never wilfully embraced a life of crime?'

The judge's tut-tuts blended with the officer's reply. 'That's my impression, sir.'

'And lastly, is it right to say that he has done everything to assist you in your task? In a word, that he has co-operated in every way?'

'Absolutely.'

There followed what, Mr Justice Pearn had to admit, was an excellent plea in mitigation. Indeed, it was so effective that instead of passing an immediate sentence of imprisonment as he had originally intended, he remanded the accused in custody for further reports on his likelihood to benefit from probation.

Afterwards he wondered if he hadn't let his heart overrule his head. But it wasn't only the plea in mitigation which had impressed him, but the police officer's candid fairness.

Arnold Feely was leaving the court well satisfied with the result when he bumped into Detective Sergeant Craddock at the main entrance.

'I didn't think you were going to get away with it,' Craddock said with a smile which was no more than a curl of the lip. He was a man of about forty, strongly built and with a face which seemed over-endowed with features, so as to give him a formidable appearance.

'I shouldn't have but for your help,' Feely replied.

Craddock gave him a small, mock bow. 'I'm still not sure that Hitler didn't have the right answer for the likes of your client. Quick extermination.' He grinned. 'But one can hardly say that in the witness-box of an English court.' Then in a throwaway tone he went on, 'I saw your wife this morning. Happened to be passing the shop and dropped in. But she was tied up with an American who seemed to want to buy everything he could see, so I didn't hang around.'

Feely accepted this piece of information without comment and soon afterwards the two men parted.

Detective Sergeant Craddock had entered the Feelys' lives two and a half years before when he had been the officer investigating a small burglary at Marcia Feely's shop near Sloane Street. He had been in and out of the shop a fair number of times after that, was soon calling Marcia Feely by her first name and generally taking an interest in her which caused her husband considerable misgivings.

But Marcia had only laughed when Feely had voiced these and had declared that it was very useful having a friend in the police.

Now, he not only called at the shop, but also at their flat for the occasional evening drink or meal. With time, Arnold Feely had managed to suppress his original feelings and had come to accept the situation.

As soon as he got back to Chambers, Feely phoned his wife at the shop. One of the two girls who assisted her part-time answered and told him that Marcia was with a Japanese customer but looked like being free in a moment or two.

'Marcia? It's me,' he said, when he heard the telephone being picked up off the cluttered desk at the back of the shop.

'Oh, hello.' Her voice sounded excited. 'I've just sold a Victorian cruet set to a Japanese gentleman for ten times what I gave for it last week. And this morning I had an American from Oklahoma who spent a thousand pounds in half an hour.'

'I heard about your American.'

'How? Oh, have you seen Sid? He looked in when the American was here.'

'I saw him at court this afternoon and he mentioned that he'd had a brief word with you.'

'Yes, we couldn't talk, so I promised I'd ring him this

evening. It'll probably be best if I ask him round for a drink. You don't mind, do you?'

'On the contrary, I think it's a good idea. I'll be back by seven, so any time after that.'

'See you later, Arnold. I must go and attend to a customer. He's one of my specials.'

CHAPTER FIVE

At half past eight the next evening, Brian said good-night to the staff still on duty, making especially sure that Talbot witnessed his departure.

'See you tomorrow, Mr Talbot,' he called out as he passed the wine steward's pantry.

Though outwardly calm, he had a disagreeable feeling in the pit of his stomach, which left him uncertain whether or not he wanted to be sick. He wished he'd not promised Fiona that he'd go back to the flat for an hour. He'd much sooner have gone to a film.

The familiar stations as he travelled west in the tube did nothing to reassure him. He felt apprehensive and vulnerable and it even crossed his mind to opt out of the whole thing. If he failed to play his allotted role, they'd be forced to abandon the plan. What then? The odds were he'd be sought out and taught a lesson. It was difficult to run away when you didn't have a clear notion of what you were running from. If Harry Green were the only person involved, there'd be no problem. But whoever it was who had singled Brian out for this enterprise knew more about him than was comfortable. No, the answer was that he'd been hooked and no amount of wriggling was going to get him off that hook. This was more apparent in retrospect than it had been at the time. It wasn't difficult to believe now that, in fact, he had never really had any choice in the matter at all.

To make things worse, when he did get back, Fiona wanted to make love and he simply wasn't in the mood. The result was she became tearful when he said he must leave again, which was a good half-hour earlier than was strictly necessary.

'Do take care, my love,' she said for the umpteenth time, tears trickling down her cheeks. 'I think I'd die if anything were to happen to you. Life is a bloody enough mess, anyway, without that.' She held his head between her two hands and gazed into his face with aching sorrow.

'I'll be all right,' he said, kissing the tip of her damp nose. 'You can cook me an enormous breakfast when I get back tomorrow morning.'

'Yes, that's just what I shall do,' she said enthusiastically. 'We'll have a real fry-up.'

'Better make sure the fire extinguisher's working first,' he remarked, kissing her again.

Fiona's cooking was inclined to be as impulsive as it was elementary and it was not uncommon for flames to leap menacingly ceilingwards whenever she used the small gas ring over in one corner of their room.

It was with a feeling of relief that he regained the pavement outside and headed back towards the underground station. He suddenly realised that coping with Fiona's emotional demands had made him forget his own sense of tension. Unfortunately, sitting alone in a half-empty train brought back all his forebodings about what lay ahead.

On the spur of the moment, he decided to alight at Piccadilly Circus and walk through to Leicester Square in the hope that the bright lights might distract his mind.

Half-way along he noticed an old lady sitting in a doorway holding out one or two sprigs of white heather. People passed by ignoring her and she, for her part, returned the compliment. Her face was wrinkled not so much from age as from neglect, and the hand which proffered the heather was gnarled and blackened as though it had been recovered from a fire.

Almost shyly, Brian approached her. 'How much for a piece?' he asked diffidently. The closer one got, the more forbidding she seemed.

She peered up at him through rheumy eyes.

'Want a bit of heather for luck, son?' she said, as if she'd not heard him in the first place.

'Please. How much?'

'Five pissing p's,' she said, giving him a grin which revealed two teeth, one at each side of her mouth like strangers who'd never met.

'Here's ten,' he said, handing her the coin and taking the sprig from her claw-like hand.

'You're a good boy,' she said, thrusting the money quickly out of sight through the layers of her clothing. 'It'll bring you luck, son, because you're a good boy. Your mum proud of you, is she?'

'She's dead.'

'She must be proud of a son like you,' she repeated. 'Not like all this lot round here,' she remarked, waving a contemptuous hand at the immediate passers-by. 'Look at 'em,' she went on, raising her voice to a near shout. 'Riff-raff, that's what they are! Look at them girls! Knickerless riff-raff!'

The two mini-skirted girls, who had been singled out for denunciation, reacted with a mixture of indignation and alarm and quickened their step.

'Don't you go wasting your time on girls like that, son. You look after your mum and make her proud of you, like she is.'

'I must be on my way,' Brian said. 'Good luck to you, too, lady.'

A little farther on he entered one of the innumerable cheap eating places in the area and ordered himself a fried egg sandwich and a large cup of black coffee. The café was packed with young people, mostly younger than Brian himself and mostly foreign. There were girls of fourteen and fifteen, obviously waiting to be picked up, and predatory males with Mediterranean complexions circling round them.

Brian watched them with detached interest. God knows he was neither saint nor yet old himself, but he found the scene depressing not so much for its sordidness as for its superficial emptiness.

It was half past ten when he left the café and, picking his way along Garrick Street and round the back of Covent Garden market, he headed straight for the Blackstone. Southampton Row was the only major thoroughfare he had to cross and he found himself making it in a dash as though some creature of prey would swoop on him if he lingered.

The narrow streets round the club were always completely deserted at this hour of night and poorly lit as well.

There were a number of darkened doorways on the opposite side to the Blackstone and Brian chose one of these in which to hide himself and spy out the land.

In a quarter of an hour's time, Talbot would be locking the main door. The place already looked deserted. There was only one light on in the upstairs room in which guests were entertained after dinner and the smoking-room was in darkness. It could be that the last member and his guests had already departed. Brian had taken the precaution of examining the list earlier in the day and had observed that only four members had booked in guests for that evening.

Leaving his hiding place, he ran across the road and, hugging the wall, made his way along to the entrance to the club. Cautiously he peered round the edge of the doorway, from where he could see into the hall and part of the way up the stairs.

There was no one in sight and, taking a deep breath, he stealthily entered. As he passed the now empty front porter's box, the telephone started to ring. His first panic reaction was to retreat rapidly into the street, but, with a pounding heart, he made himself go forward and a few seconds later he had flattened himself against the smoking-room doorway.

The phone seemed to go on ringing for ever, but eventually Talbot appeared from the direction of the kitchen bearing his glass of hot milk which he put down on a small table at the foot of the staircase.

Brian gulped. It was almost unbelievable that it was actually happening as intended. He heard Talbot answer the phone and a little later the old boy re-crossed his line of vision as he made his way upstairs to look for the forgotten handbag.

Brian experienced another moment of panic when he was unable to find the sleeping pill, but it turned out he'd put it in another pocket.

It took less than a couple of seconds to nip out from his hiding-place, drop the pill into the glass of milk and scurry back to safety again.

It was several minutes before Talbot returned downstairs empty-handed. Brian heard him hang up the phone and then lock the main door. He re-crossed Brian's line of vision once more and started to mount the stairs, taking his milk with him.

Brian gave an involuntary jump as the whole place was suddenly plunged into darkness. After that, there was the sound of a distant door closing, followed by a silence broken only by a brisk series of inanimate noises which did nothing to quieten his pulse-beat.

For several more seconds he stood stock still, hugging the security of the smoking-room doorway, then cautiously he opened the door and entered. He had been told to wait three-quarters of an hour before going up to Talbot's room and removing the keys. This would allow the old boy ample time to get into bed and for the sleeping pills to do their stuff. It was known that he didn't waste more time getting into bed than his creaking joints necessitated. At all events, Brian decided that he might as well make himself as comfortable as possible while he waited.

He chose the chair usually occupied by ex-Judge Whitby-Stansford and lowered himself gingerly into it. A little later he felt confident enough to stretch out his legs and lean back in relative relaxation. At least, he reflected, there was no danger of him falling asleep. In the event, it was the longest three-quarters of an hour he'd ever known, but at last the moment came for him to embark on the next phase of the carefully planned operation.

If the sleeping pills had worked, they should, combined with Talbot's natural deafness, have allowed a rhinoceros to have charged upstairs without disturbing him. Nevertheless, Brian mounted them slowly and with the utmost care, almost dreading the taking of each step which brought him nearer the old man's bedroom. He was thankful that he knew the geography of the upper floors as well as he did, seeing what an obstacle course it was in the dark.

He arrived outside Talbot's door and put his ear to the keyhole. His heart gave a small leap of joy as he heard the reassuring sound of snores within.

Scarcely daring to breathe himself, he turned the handle. There was a fearful creak as the door opened, but Talbot's snores mercifully continued unabated.

He tiptoed across to the head of the bed and put out a hand to locate the keys. To his intense relief he found them first time and in a matter of a couple of seconds was out of the room and closing the door. Compared with the painful slowness of his ascent, he reached the ground floor in no time at all. Passing through the swing door which led to the staff quarters, he came to the rear entrance and quickly unlocked the door.

As he did so, a figure slithered out of the shadows and was inside before the door was fully open.

'You left it bloody late getting 'ere, didn't you?' Harry Green said. 'I thought you weren't going to make it in time.'

'I did, so what are you fussing about?'

'All right! But for Christ's sake get a move on locking that door and showing me where the stuff's kept. I don't like 'anging about on a job.'

'What about my money?'

'I told you, you get it when I leave.' Harry Green's tone was anything but agreeable.

'I want to see you've got it first!'

For a moment, Brian thought he was going to make an issue out of it, but then with a snarl he shone his flashlight into the holdall he was carrying. Stacked at one end were seven bundles of fivers.

'There!' he hissed angrily. 'And if you think you're going to stop and count it, you can 'ave another bloody think. Now, for Christ's sake, let's get on.'

'Give us your torch,' Brian said. Then, as if he might have been conducting Harry Green to a seat in a cinema, he led the way to the display cases.

Brian unlocked all three and, while Green was emptying the first, he removed a snuff-box from one of the other cases and slipped it into his own pocket. It was the one over whose fate the bequests sub-committee had recently deliberated.

The whole operation occupied three or four minutes at the outside and then Harry Green was ready to be conducted downstairs again.

When they reached the rear entrance, Brian paused beside the door but made no attempt to unlock it. For a moment neither man spoke nor moved, then Green propped the holdall on a ledge and pulled out the seven bundles of notes.

'Six of 'em contain twenty fivers and one has ten,' he said by way of grudging explanation, adding viciously, 'And now unlock that bloody door!'

After Green had departed, Brian stuffed the money into the travel bag he'd brought with him and then went upstairs to replace the keys. Apart from the fact that Talbot's snores had shifted an octave, nothing had changed.

He returned to the smoking-room and spent the next quarter of an hour counting his money in the dark. He was almost surprised to find it correct.

The time was half past midnight. That meant he had seven hours to while away before Talbot came down and unlocked the rear door. He reckoned he could safely kip for a few hours, but he must ensure that he didn't oversleep. The very thought was enough to send him into a cold sweat. He kicked off his shoes, but decided to keep on the pair of cotton gloves he'd been wearing since he slipped into the club. They had been supplied by Green and Brian had noticed that he wore an identical pair.

Stretching out in the same chair as before, he soon fell asleep. It was more comfortable than a good many places he'd slept in and exhaustion saw to the rest.

When he awoke, he couldn't at first think where he was and then everything flooded back like a tap turned full on. The heavy curtains which covered the windows were etched round with the first light of a new day. He screwed up his eyes to look at his watch. It was just after seven o'clock. There were no sounds coming yet from upstairs, though it wouldn't be long before Talbot descended to make himself a cup of tea.

Brian picked up the bag he'd placed beneath the chair and had a quick feel to make sure the money was still there. Satisfied that it was, he tried to think what tell-tale marks he might have left in the dark, decided there couldn't be any and felt his way out of the room.

There were still no sounds coming from upstairs as he crossed the hall and entered the staff quarters. He had already decided that the best place to hide while awaiting the opportunity to slip out was behind the cellar door. This was close to the rear entrance of the club and wasn't somewhere Talbot was likely to go poking on his first round of the day.

For fifteen minutes or so, Brian stood there patiently, but when there was still no sound of Talbot coming, he began to get nervous. Supposing the old boy had, despite his reassuring snores, died in the night!

It was to his credit that the thought caused him as much concern on Talbot's behalf as it did on his own.

He opened the cellar door in order to look at his watch in the daylight which now filled the passage outside. It was nearly eight o'clock. And still the place was as quiet as a mausoleum.

Without any clear idea in his head as to what he was going to do, he returned along the passage and had just reached the swing-door when he thought he heard the stair creak, which was enough to send him scurrying back to his hiding-place.

He was barely there when there was the unmistakable sound of the swing-door being kicked open as Talbot made his unsteady way to the kitchen.

Brian could hear him filling a kettle with water and placing it on the stove. This was followed by the rattle of tea-cup and saucer.

Would he never unlock the back door!

Eventually, there were sounds closer to hand and through the door which was ajar Brian saw him shuffle past. He gave the impression of a sleep-walker performing something by rote. The poor old boy was probably still feeling as if he had lead weights attached to his eyelids. But at least he was alive!

Brian waited until he had gone back into the kitchen and in one swift movement he left his hiding-place, skipped on tip-toe along the five yards of passage to the back-door and let himself out. He paused only when he reached the street on to which the back yard gave. There was no one in sight and a minute or two later he was mingling with people hurrying to work along Southampton Row.

He decided to avoid Holborn Underground Station just in case one of the staff on duty there might recognise him and remember the fact because it wasn't his usual time. Instead he made his way down to the Embankment and caught a train at the Temple station. Similar caution caused him to get out at a different station the other end and to give himself a longer walk.

It was just after half past eight when he entered the house in which they had their room. Far from there being any smell of breakfast cooking, Fiona was still asleep.

She opened one eye and blinked up at him. Then like a projectile she rose from the bed, the blanket and sheet falling away from her.

'Oh, love, it's you and you're safe!' She flung her arms around his neck and burst into tears. 'I'm so relieved to see you,' she said, through sobs. 'I dreamt something awful had happened to you.'

'What?'

'It doesn't matter now you're here. I don't want to think about it.'

He reached into his pocket and brought out the snuff-box. For a second she looked at it uncomprehending. Then her face lit up.

'Absolutely perfect!' she crowed, turning it over in her hand. 'It's such a delicious idea!'

CHAPTER SIX

As he approached the Blackstone Club three hours later, Brian experienced an even greater nervousness than he had the previous night. It was the realisation that he mustn't give himself away by a slip of the tongue or by appearing in any way different from usual.

The only thing he could be sure of was that the theft must have been discovered by now and presumably the place would be swarming with police.

As he turned the handle of the back door, he braced himself against the unexpected. He was scarcely inside when a man not much older than himself and with suspicious grey eyes barred his way.

'Who are you?'

Brian affected innocent surprise.

'Brian Tanner. I work here. Why, what's up?'

The other consulted a list which he had clipped to a millboard. 'Assistant wine steward?'

'S'right.'

The man's expression became less unfriendly.

'There's been a burglary. Someone's knocked off all your snuff-boxes.'

'Cor! They must be worth quite a bit.'

'You should know!' Brian felt a slow flush begin to suffuse his face and couldn't believe that it wasn't obvious to the officer who added casually, 'Working here, I mean.'

'I've not been here all that time.'

'You'd better have a word with Detective Sergeant Ellis. That's him there by the kitchen door. Hey, Sarge, this is one of the staff who's just arrived. Name of Tanner. Assistant wine steward.'

Sergeant Ellis beckoned Brian to him and then led the way into the wine pantry. Muttering 'Tanner, Tanner,' to himself, he sorted through a sheaf of papers.

'Yes, here we are, Brian Tanner, assistant wine steward,' he said, extracting a sheet of foolscap and placing it on top of the others. 'What time did you go off duty yesterday, Brian?' he enquired in a pleasantly conversational tone.

'Half past eight.'

'Half past eight,' Sergeant Ellis repeated slowly, writing it down.

'Come back again later?'

'Later last night, you mean?'

'Yup, that's what I mean.'

'No. I had no reason to.'

'Had no reason to,' Sergeant Ellis repeated as he made a note.

His manner was jaunty, but Brian found it dangerously so.

'Where'd you spend the evening?'

'With my girl-friend.'

'Her name?'

'Fiona. Fiona Richey.' Brian's tone was uncertain. Why hadn't he anticipated this? He felt as if he were standing on the threshold of a trap. One untoward move and it would suddenly close on him.

'Presumably she'll be able to confirm that, if necessary?' Sergeant Ellis said, looking up from his notes.

'Of course,' Brian replied trying to sound more convincing than he felt.

'Well, that's really all for the moment, Brian. We may want to ask you a few more questions later and we'll probably get this down in a short statement for you to sign.' He glanced at the rows of bottles. 'Is this where you work?'

'Yes. Talbot and I. Incidentally, is Mr Talbot all right?'

'Why shouldn't he be?' Sergeant Ellis asked, fixing him with a quizzical look.

'Only that he sleeps here. He's the only one who does.'

'So I understand. No, he's all right. He's with Detective Chief Superintendent Samson at the moment.' Observing Brian's expression, he smiled and said, 'You didn't think I was in charge of the whole enquiry, did you?'

'I didn't know.'

'Don't mind if I make this my personal headquarters, do you?'

'Not a bit. Have a drink?'

'What! With a Chief Super, a Chief Inspector and a D.I. all within sniffing distance, are you joking! Anyway, are you allowed to give away the club's liquor like that?'

'I'm sure the secretary wouldn't mind in the circumstances.'

'The answer's still no. Thanks all the same.' He smothered a yawn. 'There's no reason why you shouldn't be getting on with whatever you're supposed to be doing. We can't help our presence being seen, but we're not meant to disturb the members. It's not like when we raid a Soho night-club,' he added with a chuckle. 'Then it's grab everyone and everything in sight. But the Blackstone Club's a kid gloves job. Treat everyone with the same respect as if you're all in court together. Incidentally, is it right that Mr Justice Pearn is chairman of the committee?' Brian nodded and Sergeant Ellis continued, 'He gave me a roasting last time I appeared in his court. Just because he got something arseways up, he took it out of me. Judges are apt to do that in my experience. Suppose I'd recognise a good many familiar faces amongst your members! Not that I want to try.'

'How'd the burglar get into the club?' Brian asked, deciding to take advantage of Sergeant Ellis' chatty mood.

'That's a good question! He either had a set of keys or it was an inside job.'

'It couldn't have been an inside job!'

'Couldn't have been?' Sergeant Ellis echoed.

'Mr Talbot's the only person who sleeps on the premises and it's daft to think he had anything to do with it.'

'That's apparently what everyone's saying. Loyal servant of the club for over forty years etcetera etcetera. Unthinkable! Terrible suggestion!' He gave Brian a look of wry amusement. 'You don't have to be in the police for long to realise that nothing's unthinkable. But nothing! Anyway, whatever your Mr Talbot did or didn't do, he has a few spiky questions to answer.'

At that moment one of the waitresses appeared in the doorway of the pantry.

'Hello, Brian,' she said in a scared voice. 'What's up?'

'There's been a burglary, that's all.'

'Yes, that's all!' Sergeant Ellis chimed in genially. 'Now, what's your name, my dear?'

Leaving the officer shuffling through his papers preparatory to asking the girl the routine questions he'd just been answering, Brian made his way to the smoking-room.

It was empty, which wasn't surprising as the club didn't officially open until noon and it was only a few minutes past that hour. Moreover, it was between half past twelve and one that the majority of those intending to have lunch came in. It was only one or two of the older retired members, such as ex-Judge Whitby-Stansford, who timed their arrival with the opening of the main door.

Brian stood just inside the door and gazed about him with an air of unreality. It was difficult to believe that this was where he had spent most of last night. Now, it was the familiar smoking-room again. Was it really in here that he had wrestled with early panic, made worse by the darkness and all the unpredictable sounds of an old building settling down for the night?

His glance alighted on the chair in which he had slept. Something beneath it caught his eye and he moved closer to see what it was. But he already knew and his heart was pounding as he dived his hand down to retrieve the small sprig of white heather that lay there.

Even as he thrust it into his trouser pocket, the door opened and the secretary came in followed by two men who were obviously police officers.

He gave Brian a nod and said, 'I've arranged for something cold to be sent up to my room for lunch for Sir John and myself and these gentlemen. You might see that a carafe of white burgundy is put on the tray.'

'Certainly, sir.'

'That's Tanner, Talbot's assistant,' Brian heard Colonel Tatham say, as he was leaving the room.

By the time that most of the members had arrived for lunch, the police had managed to complete their examination of the public rooms and had tactfully retreated out of sight.

It was inevitable, however, that word of what had happened spread even more rapidly than a bush fire fanned by a breeze and the empty display cases became a focus of gazes which ranged from the stupefied to the near reverential.

There were a few whose comments inclined towards the cynical, but most expressed outrage at what one member aptly referred to as a deed of plunder.

Around two o'clock, Smith, the head waiter, asked Brian to take a tray of food up to Talbot in his room.

'He's not feeling very well,' he said, 'and Colonel Tatham has advised him to rest.' As Brian was departing on this mission, Smith added, 'Better take him up a tot of brandy. I think he could probably use it.'

As he mounted the final flight of stairs which led to Talbot's room, Brian was again overcome with a feeling of cloying unreality at the different circumstances which now took him there.

He knocked on the door. There was a faint 'come-in' and he entered.

Talbot was lying on his bed, hands folded across his midriff, looking as if he were expecting the undertaker rather than a tray of food.

'Hello, Brian,' he said weakly, turning his head.

'How are you feeling? I've brought you something to eat. There's also some brandy.'

'Brandy? Yes, I could do with a little brandy.'

Brian put the tray down on the bedside table and handed him the glass. Talbot took it and, propping himself up on one elbow, downed it in one.

'I don't mind telling you, Brian, I've had a terrible experience with that dreadful man this morning.'

'Which man is that?'

'That Superintendent Samson! He made shocking suggestions. As good as accused me of stealing the club's property! I said to him, "If you think I've done that, you'd better speak to Sir John because he'll soon tell you how wrong you are".'

'And what did he say to that?'

'Just said they had to make their enquiries.' Talbot sank back on his pillow. 'He's a dreadful man and I don't mind who knows it,' he added with a shudder. 'I shall ask Sir John to see that I don't have to speak to him again.'

'Were you able to tell the police anything?' Brian asked, trying not to make his tone sound too eager.

'All I could tell them was that I slept soundly all night and didn't hear a thing.'

'The burglar must have had a set of duplicate keys, I suppose.'

'That dreadful man kept on and on about keys. All I could tell him was that mine never left my possession. They even questioned me about my sleeping pills and about my glass of milk. Wanted to see the glass! I don't know what they thought that'd tell them. Particularly, after I'd washed it up, like I always do as soon as I come down in the morning.'

Brian breathed a silent sigh of relief. It seemed that the sprig of white heather had lived up to its reputation, even to the extent of drawing attention to itself under the smoking-room chair.

Talbot turned his head and Brian observed, to his embarrassment, a large tear trickling down the old man's cheek.

'I love the Blackstone,' the old man said in a choked voice. 'It's been my only love since my dear wife's death. As if I'd steal its property! It'd be like stealing from myself. That dreadful man and his insinuations!'

'I'd better get back downstairs,' Brian said awkwardly. 'Is there anything else you'd like?'

Talbot cast a disdainful look at the tray of food. 'You can take that away,' he said, 'and bring me another brandy.' As Brian was going out of the door, he added in something like his old voice, 'And you can tell them I shall stay in my room until that dreadful man has left!'

Brian returned downstairs with mixed feelings. He was relieved to find out personally that nothing worse than Talbot's dignity had suffered. On the other hand, however, the senior wine steward was clearly under police suspicion and this troubled Brian's conscience in a manner he'd not anticipated. He tried to think of something he could do which would put Talbot indisputably in the clear. Something, that is, which wouldn't at the same time incriminate himself. But, for the moment, he could think of nothing.

When he reached the ground floor, he was upbraided

for having been so long and was told he was required in the smoking-room immediately. Smith, the head waiter, said a trifle testily that he would take Talbot his further tot of brandy when he had a moment to spare.

Thereafter, the day for Brian resumed a normal course. The club emptied as usual soon after lunch, apart from the few ancient siesta takers, and half the staff went off duty for a couple of hours. Brian noticed that ex-Judge Whitby-Stansford was not in his customary chair—or, indeed, in any other—and he wondered vaguely what had befallen the grumpy old man. Normally, only fog or snow kept him away.

About half past four, Sir John Pearn came hurrying into the club and went straight upstairs to the secretary's room. Shortly afterwards, the bell in the wine pantry rang and Brian went there in answer to the summons.

Apart from Sir John and Colonel Tatham, the only other person present was Detective Chief Superintendent Samson. Brian was told to fetch them some tea. When he returned, they were sitting round the table in an obvious council of war. He would dearly have liked to have remained as a fly on the wall. After all, he was as interested as anyone—possibly more so—in knowing what had happened to the snuff-boxes. One thing for certain, they must have passed out of Harry Green's possession by now.

As soon as Brian had left the room, Sir John Pearn turned to Detective Chief Superintendent Samson and said, 'Well, officer, I understand you wished to see me again.'

Chief Superintendent Samson nodded. He felt a spark of resentment at being addressed as 'officer', as though he were a young P.C. giving evidence in a motoring case, but determined not to show it. He was equally determined not to address Sir John as 'my lord' as he would do were they in court.

'This, sir,' he said, clearing his throat, 'was obviously

45

a professional job, well-planned and carefully executed by someone who had inside knowledge—if not inside help. No fingerprints were left and so far we've not been able to find any clues at all. As I said earlier, sir, one of two things happened. Either Talbot assisted in the theft by admitting the thief and then letting him out again *or* someone managed to obtain a duplicate set of the club's keys.'

'Impossible,' Colonel Tatham said sharply. 'At least, impossible that it could have been my set. And you have Talbot's word that his set have never been out of his possession.'

Chief Superintendent Samson sighed. It had been his common experience as a C.I.D. officer that people frequently adopted set attitudes in the course of an investigation and then refused to budge, even when confronted by facts.

'Has there never been any occasion when you have parted with your keys? For example, mightn't someone at some time have wished to borrow them for one purpose or another?' Samson's tone was cajoling. He knew that if he sounded remotely censorious, all he'd get would be a flat denial.

'They've certainly never been out of my possession for more than a few minutes,' he said stiffly. 'I may have lent them to the head waiter or the porter on the front door for some specific purpose.'

Samson nodded encouragingly. 'And when you've been away, for example?'

'They've been held by Collins. He keeps the books and is a sort of chief clerk.'

It was as Samson had suspected, though he was tactful enough not to reveal any sign of triumph at the extraction of this admission.

'What would certainly be most helpful,' he said patiently, 'would be if you and Talbot would list on a piece of paper all the occasions you can recall parting with your keys and to whom.'

'Over what sort of period?' Colonel Tatham asked grumpily.

'Say, over the last two months.'

'I don't know how I'm expected to remember that!'

'But I gathered it didn't happen very often,' Samson observed mildly, 'so it shouldn't be too difficult.'

'It's not the sort of detail one records in one's diary you know!'

'Still, I'm sure you'll do your best. It could prove very important.' Samson's smile was sweet, though his tone now had a discernibly steely edge.

'Are you suggesting that the keys were copied on one of these occasions when the secretary—or Talbot if he ever did—parted with their bunch?' Sir John Pearn asked with judicial gravity.

'It's a possibility that I have to explore, sir. It doesn't take very long to copy keys if they've been borrowed for that specific purpose.'

Sir John pursed his lips. 'Well, we'll obviously do our best to assist,' he said in a voice which made it clear that he was chairing the meeting. 'What's the next matter you wish to mention?'

'It's the question of the disposal of the snuff-boxes,' Samson said in a slowly thoughtful tone. 'The point being that they're not easily disposable. Somebody's sitting on over twenty thousand pounds worth of snuff-boxes. They can't be melted down like gold bars and re-appear in different form. They can't be broken into separate untraceable items like a valuable pendant or a necklace. They are, and remain, snuff-boxes, identifiable and almost certain to be spotted as soon as they appear in public.'

'So?' Sir John said in the pause which followed.

'They've either gone straight into someone's private collection, or they'll be individually sold to known private

collectors, some of whom, we know, are notoriously un-
concerned to enquire about the source of their purchases.
Acquisition is everything to them and you don't ask too
many questions.'

'It shouldn't be too difficult to find out the names of
those who have such collections,' Sir John said. 'They'd
be known to the dealers and probably to museums, like
the Victoria and Albert.'

'I agree, sir,' Samson said. 'Another possibility is that
they'll be smuggled out of the country and sold abroad.
That'd probably be as safe and lucrative a method of
disposal as any.'

'Is there a known foreign market for English snuff-
boxes?' Sir John enquired intently.

'That's something I can find out, sir.' Samson paused,
aware that his next observation was likely to produce outrage. 'I am wondering if you have any known collectors
amongst your own members?'

'Good gracious! What an astonishing suggestion!' Sir
John said, while Colonel Tatham shook his head as though
he couldn't have heard aright.

'As I said earlier, sir, collectors of *objets d'art* are liable
to have blind spots when it comes to their determination
to acquire a particular item.'

'Don't let's mince our words,' Sir John said severely.
'What you're saying is that certain people in that class
allow their cupidity to overcome their sense of honesty.'

'Precisely, sir.'

'Anyway, to return to your suggestion that a member of
this club might be such a person.' He glanced at the secretary. 'I suppose we have a fair number of collectors of one
sort or another, though I don't know of anyone who
specialises in snuff-boxes, do you, Tatham?'

The secretary shook his head. 'I find it hard to believe
that a member of the Blackstone would perpetrate such a
despicable crime against the club,' he said, with a wintry

expression. 'Apart from anything else, he'd be running such a risk!'

'I don't follow that last bit, sir,' Samson said. 'After all, a few moments ago, you were pouring scorn on the suggestion that any of your members could be involved.'

Colonel Tatham retreated into silence behind a portentous frown, and Sir John said quickly, 'I suppose you would like a list of members who are known to have collections of *objets d'art*.'

'It would be helpful, sir.'

'Of course, it would have to be treated in strictest confidence.'

'It would be.'

'And also be the subject of certain undertakings as to the use made of it.'

'I don't think that would present any difficulty, sir.'

'Very well, I'll discuss the matter further with the secretary and we'll let you know what we can do.'

'I'm obliged, sir.'

'The club's only interest is the return of its property and to see the prosecution of those involved in this dastardly crime.'

'Naturally, sir. I hope we shall be able to achieve both ends.'

Sir John rose to indicate that he regarded their meeting as closed.

'I take it there's nothing else you wish to bring up at the moment?' he said, as an afterthought.

'No, I think I've covered about everything, sir. For the time being, that is.'

'Any thoughts on what your next move'll be?' Sir John asked in a faintly patronising tone, as he moved towards the door.

'Yes, quite a few, sir,' Samson said amiably.

Sir John paused expectantly for a fraction of a second, only to make a dignified exit when it was obvious that De-

tective Chief Superintendent Samson had no intention of
being more forthcoming.

CHAPTER SEVEN

A strong and not particularly enticing smell of cooking
greeted Brian's nostrils as he neared the door of their
room that evening.

Inside Fiona was sitting on the bed, hunched over a
paperback which lay on her lap. Over in the corner of
the room smoke was rising from an open pan on the gas
ring.

'Hello, love,' she said, leaping up and giving Brian a
kiss. 'I never heard you open the door.'

'Something's burning.'

'I think it's all right,' she said doubtfully, going across
and giving it a half-hearted stir with a bent fork.

Brian glanced down at the book which had been absorbing her attention. *Concepts of a Freed Society* by A. Jawal,
he read. She was always reading things with titles such as
that, which meant absolutely nothing to him. Early on in
their relationship, she had tried to get him interested in
some of the high-flown stuff she read, to infect him with
her enthusiasm. But he had made it clear that this was not
an aspect of her life which he had any wish to share. At
first, however, she had taken his indifference for shyness
or modesty and it was only when he flatly said he didn't
want his mind spoilt for Mickey Spillane that she gave
up.

He watched her, as with the utmost concentration, she

began to spoon the contents of the pan on to two plates. It seemed that a fair amount was adhering to the bottom of the pan and had to be prised off in flakes and lumps and this required all her attention.

He didn't often stop to wonder what it was about her that attracted him. It certainly had nothing to do with her intellect or the fact that she had had a university education or came from a higher reach of society. None of those things mattered to him in the slightest.

It wasn't that she was stunningly pretty or had a terrific figure. Indeed, she was slightly plump and had a funny little pug nose, though she had a nice complexion. There was certainly something attractive to Brian about her wide mouth which somehow symbolised her vitality. And it was this almost animal vitality which had fascinated him. Having grown up against the background of a broken home and passed through the difficult years of adolescence generally starved of affection, he had been subconsciously ready for a bit of mothering, provided it was not too cloying.

At all events, Fiona was the first girl with whom he had ever spent more than a casual night and whose company brought him more than mere sexual solace.

'Here, love, take this,' she said, handing him the plate on which she had heaped the larger portion.

'What is it?'

'Paella.'

'What the hell's that?'

'It's a Spanish dish.'

When they were seated side by side on the bed, he said, 'I told the police I was with you all last night. I hadn't meant to drag you in, but they asked me where I'd spent the night and I said with my girl-friend.' His tone was apologetic.

'Well, that's all right, love. What are you worried about? If they ask me, I'll tell them we were here together all night. No one knows otherwise, so there's no problem.'

'You won't mind then if the police get in touch with you?'

Her fork paused half-way to her mouth and she looked thoughtful.

'I'd prefer not to have them around,' she said, slowly, 'but it probably doesn't matter all that much.' Her expression brightened. 'Anyway, giving you an alibi is the most important thing.'

'It'll only be a routine check on their part as they have no reason to suspect me of anything.'

She nodded keenly. 'Of course I don't mind. I don't see what else you could have done. And if the police do come, I needn't tell the others.'

Brian gave a small sigh of relief. 'Thanks for being so understanding.'

'You never thought I'd let you down, did you?'

'No, but I'm still sorry I had to drag you in. They took me by surprise asking me my movements.'

She put out a hand and gave his cheek an affectionate pat.

'How much longer do you think you'll stay at the Blackstone?' she asked after a pause.

'It'd look a bit odd if I left now.'

'Oh, I don't think you should.'

'And, anyway, aren't you forgetting why I went there in the first place?'

'Of course I'm not forgetting, love. You're helping us by being there.'

'So you like to pretend. It doesn't seem to me I'm much bloody help.'

'But you are and will go on being. It's very important to have people in the right places.' Her voice was eager. 'We were discussing this the other evening and everyone agreed.' She glanced at her watch. 'I have to go out in a few minutes.'

'Another meeting?'

She nodded. 'But I shan't be late.'

'Hmm! I know your lot. Most of them can't stop talking once they start and it doesn't take much to get them started.'

Fiona smothered a giggle. 'I remember now, there was something I had to ask you. Is there a judge in your club called Pearn?'

'He's the chairman. I've told you about him. You see! You don't even listen when I do tell you things!'

'Oh, love, I do. I knew his name sounded familiar. I just wanted to confirm.'

'Anyway, why do you ask?'

'Oh, they just told me to find out from you.'

'And you're not going to tell me any more?'

'There's nothing more to tell, love,' she said, refusing to meet his gaze.

She jumped up from the bed, seized her shaggy coat, kissed him quickly on the forehead and dashed out of the room.

Brian reached for a cigarette and for the next few minutes lay back against the wall with a thoughtful expression as he smoked.

The matter which preoccupied his mind was what to do with the seven hundred and fifty pounds which at the moment lay in a bag beneath their bed.

If the police called to check on his story, they might well take the opportunity of being nosy and if they should then find the money, there'd be some difficult questions to answer.

If he gave it to Fiona for safe keeping, she'd probably hide it at the place where they held their meetings. And though he trusted her, he didn't extend his trust to the others.

In the end he decided to think of a hiding-place in their bedroom. After all, if the police came making a mere routine check, they'd scarcely turn the place over. So provided it was right out of sight, it'd be O.K.

With this resolved, he got up and set about washing the plates in the small basin. Leaving the pan to soak, he decided to go off to the local for a pint of beer.

CHAPTER EIGHT

Two days later, a number of separate things happened all within a short space of time.

Relating the events chronologically, the first concerned Mr Justice Pearn.

He arrived at the Royal Courts of Justice on the dot of ten o'clock, it being his custom to arrive at least half an hour before he was due to sit in court. He strode briskly along the judges' corridor until he came to the heavy oak door beside which his name was boldly painted in black letters.

His clerk was already there, fussing at the cupboard in which his various sets of judicial robes were kept.

'Good morning, Robert,' Mr Justice Pearn said affably.

'Good morning, my lord. Do you wish to robe immediately?'

'No. Come back in twenty minutes. I've got a couple of letters I want to write. You can post them when I've gone into court.'

'I've put your mail on the desk, my lord.'

Mr Justice Pearn glanced across at the small pile of letters which awaited his attention. The mail he received at court fell broadly into two categories. Circulars and letters from the mentally unbalanced. Amongst the latter, there was also the occasional anonymous letter of abuse.

On this particular morning, there was a catalogue from a firm of legal publishers, a leaflet setting out the benefits of a new insurance scheme for the over sixties which he dropped disdainfully into the wastepaper basket and a letter addressed to him personally, if incorrectly.

The envelope was typewritten and bore a stamp which had been stuck on at an untidy angle. It read:

> 'Justice Pearn.
> Law Courts.
> London.'

He frowned. He didn't like being incorrectly addressed, even by cranks. Picking up a small tortoiseshell paper knife, he slit the envelope and extracted a single sheet of folded paper. This read:

> 'We understand you have been picked to try the case of Gregor Maltby at Old Bailey next week. We think you're prejudiced and another judge should take the case. Please give this very serious consideration.'

He read it through a second time, causing him to frown more heavily. It was not unknown for judges to receive threatening letters, particularly when they were involved in cases of notoriety and more particularly still if they were concerned in one having a political flavour, but it was the first time he personally had received a letter which was both threatening and sane.

Gregor Maltby was a young man who had for some time been a self-appointed thorn in the flesh of various authorities. The case which brought him to the Old Bailey involved his incitement of a group of coloured immigrants to barricade themselves in a newly completed wing of some council offices in East London. Inevitably, their eviction had led to assaults on, and by, those trying to get them out and also to a fair amount of damage to property.

So far as Mr Justice Pearn was concerned, however, Maltby and three others were up on straightforward criminal charges and he had no intention of allowing the trial to become a platform for the expounding of political views. He supposed that was what the writers of the letter meant by 'prejudiced'.

He sat down with a sigh. As if he hadn't enough things on his mind at the moment. A High Court judge's life was arduous enough in its own right. Then there was the theft from the Blackstone. And now this.

It wasn't that he was frightened by the letter, but obviously the police would have to be informed and that meant additional bother. There'd be strict security arrangements for the trial for a start and some wretched young P.C. would be instructed to keep a watch on his home.

He groaned aloud. And on top of it all, the grossly ill-informed public firmly believed that he and his brethren on the Bench were under-employed and over-paid.

By a curious coincidence, Arnold Feely also received an anonymous letter by first post that morning, though it was one of a quite different nature. The coincidence aspect was emphasised by the fact that he had been briefed to defend one of Gregor Maltby's co-defendants.

Normally, Feely went straight to court in the morning, but on this particular day he had a case which was listed 'not before twelve o'clock' and decided to spend an hour or so in chambers drafting an opinion that was overdue.

He had been at his desk about half an hour when the junior clerk came in and said breezily, 'Here you are, Mr Feely, someone's written you a fan letter.'

He handed Feely an envelope on which his name and

chambers address had been typewritten. For a second, Feely had frozen, but then he had taken the unopened letter from the clerk and had put it down on his desk with a murmur of thanks.

As soon as the clerk had left the room, he slit it open carefully and pulled out the plain piece of paper inside. He stared at it expressionless for a full minute and then with equal care refolded the note and returned it to its envelope. Taking a key from his trouser pocket, he unlocked a drawer of his desk and put the letter in. Not on top, but at the back beneath some business papers. After re-locking the drawer, he went across to the window and stared out. Every word of the note he had just read was imprinted on his mind.

It had read:

'Why don't you keep a closer eye on your wife?'

In point of time, it was while Arnold Feely was still staring thoughtfully out of the window that Detective Sergeant Craddock turned into the street where Marcia Feely had her shop.

From the window it appeared empty and he imagined that she was in the small office at the back. He was about to enter when she suddenly emerged from behind a large piece of furniture followed by an elderly man who was obviously a customer.

She suddenly caught sight of him through the door and made a quick motion to him not to come in. The customer appeared not to notice what was going on and Marcia Feely steered his attention to some object which required him to turn his back on the door.

Sergeant Craddock hastened away from the door and walked on down the street. A quarter of an hour later, from a vantage point about fifty yards from the shop, he saw the customer leave and set off in the opposite direction.

When he was lost to sight, Craddock retraced his steps and, this time, went straight into the shop.

Marcia Feely was obviously expecting him. 'Sorry to head you off like that,' she said, 'but that old boy is a member of Arnold's club.'

'The Blackstone?'

'Where else!'

'Who is he?'

'He's a retired judge. Name of Whitby-Stansford. Has pots of money. Not that he's given to throwing it about. Not in my shop, at any rate! He's usually trying to sell me something.'

'Does he know who you are?'

'I don't think he does. I've never told him. I only know he's a member because I've heard Arnold mention his name.'

'What did he want today?' Craddock asked with a note of suspicion.

'He never reached the point of saying. He just seemed to want to prowl around. I'm not clear why he came in.'

'Are you alone?'

'Yes. Georgina has a cold and isn't coming in. I shall be on my own all day.'

He glanced over her shoulder towards the office. 'Can we go in there?'

Without a word, she led the way into the tiny cluttered room. He closed the door behind them.

That same morning, Brian arrived at the Blackstone Club a few minutes after eleven o'clock. From the fact that Talbot was in evidence downstairs again, Brian deduced that Detective Chief Superintendent Samson was not on the premises. This turned out to be the case, though he was soon informed by Talbot that Detective Sergeant Ellis was in the snuff-room interviewing various members of the staff.

'He's more like a gentleman,' Talbot remarked. 'Very different from that dreadful man who was here the other day.'

'Are the police on to anything yet?' Brian asked.

'No. And if you ask me, they never will be. The Blackstone has said good-bye to its collection of snuff-boxes.'

Talbot's tone was emphatic and he spoke as if it almost gave him satisfaction to make such a prophesy. But before Brian could ask him any further questions, he bustled out, leaving Brian to get on with decanting wine for lunch.

It was while he was still doing this that one of the waitresses stuck her head round the door.

'You're wanted on the phone, Brian,' she said and disappeared again. It was as well, as the news gave him such a start that he spilt some wine and began to tremble violently.

When he reached the phone, it was several seconds before he could bring himself to pick the receiver up.

'Hello,' he said in a voice which sounded as though his throat had been sand-papered.

'Is that Brian?'

'Yes.'

'It's me, you know who!'

Brian had, indeed, at once recognised Harry Green's familiar tones.

'What do you want?'

'I want to see you.'

'What for?'

'I can't explain that on the phone. But something's cropped up. We got to meet. What time are you off this evening?'

'Half past seven.'

'Come to forty-two 'Ersholt Street. It's near Euston.'

'I don't know . . .'

'You got to come. It's for your own good.'

'How do you mean?'

'Look, I can't stop 'ere answering questions. I'll expect you around eight o'clock. Now you've got the address, 'aven't you?'

'Forty-two Hersholt Street,' Brian said as though the words were being sucked out of him against his will.

'That's right.' Harry Green's tone was impatient and the next second the line went dead.

Happily the club was unusually busy that day—news of the theft had brought in quite a few members who seldom appeared—and Brian had less time to ponder his coming meeting than would otherwise have been the case. Nevertheless, as he plied between the wine steward's pantry and the smoking-room his mind was never far away from the matter. But the more he thought about it, the more bemused he became.

What on earth could have happened to cause Harry Green to phone him as he had? It certainly wasn't any ties of friendship. Moreover, this time the meeting was to be at a private address, not at the café where they'd met on the two previous occasions. What was to be made of that? For some reason, Harry Green didn't wish to be seen out. But why not, if that was, in fact, so?

Maybe something had fouled up the subsequent plans, not that Green had sounded in any panic. Rather the contrary, his tone had been businesslike, almost peremptory.

The one possibility that loomed uppermost in his mind was that it was some sort of trap. But with what object? If Green imagined he was going to arrive at 42 Hersholt Street with £750 in his pocket which would then be forcibly taken off him ... Not even Harry Green could think he'd be so stupid. So what? The snuff-boxes must have been spirited well away by now, so it wouldn't be anything to do with them.

The longer he pondered, the less satisfactory answers he came up with. Finally, it occurred to him that Green was proposing to seek his partnership in some further enterprise. It seemed unlikely, given the terms on which they had parted company last time, but he supposed it was possible that Green had another venture in mind for which he, Brian, was especially qualified.

In the circumstances, it was with a mixture of relief and apprehension that he went off duty that evening. Before leaving, he studied the club's street map of London to ascertain exactly where Hersholt Street lay. It was about half a mile north east of the main line railway station. He decided to go by underground and get out at Euston.

In the event, it was easier to find than he'd expected and he had to ask the way only once.

Hersholt Street ran between two busier thoroughfares. There were Victorian terraced houses on both sides and one or two small shops and a pub at one end. It had a seedy air and was just the sort of street Brian would have expected Harry Green to live in. It hadn't come down in the world: it had never been up.

Finding himself on the side of the odd numbers, he crossed over. There was number 8, then number 10, then number 12. He quickened his pace, glancing from time to time at the numbers painted, for the most part, on glass panels over the front doors. Number 28, number 30; he was getting close. As he passed number 36, he glanced ahead to pick out what must obviously be number 42.

It looked little different from its neighbours. Perhaps a bit more neglected, that was all. A yellow light shone through the grimy glass above the front door and the 4 and the 2 had flaked partially off.

Brian sought a bell, but was unable to find one and eventually seized the old-fashioned iron knocker on the door and gave a good resounding knock. So good, in fact, that the door swung back a few inches and he saw that the catch was broken. He found himself looking into a short narrow hall which was devoid of any furniture. On the floor was ancient brown linoleum which also covered the stairs except where it was worn completely through.

Brian stepped inside and pushed the door to behind him. The front room on the right was in darkness, as was the kitchen beyond it. But the fact of the hall light being on seemed to indicate that someone was at home.

Standing at the bottom of the stairs, he called out 'Harry' in a voice which trembled. There was no response and in a slightly bolder tone, he tried again.

'Is Harry Green there?'

But he was met only by silence and was on the point of going when a drop of liquid fell on his head. He looked up sharply and a second drop caught him on the cheek, and then, as he stepped back, a series of drops splashed down on the bottom stair.

A quick examination revealed it to be water. Water overflowing from somewhere upstairs. He had a sudden picture of Harry Green drowning in a bath.

Taking the stairs two at a time, he reached the landing and saw the water was coming from beneath the door of the room over the kitchen. At the moment it was no more than a growing trickle. As he stared at it, a small fish came floating out. It gave him a forlorn look as it got edged across the floor towards its death fall below.

Brian flung open the door and gazed at the scene within. The floor was covered with water and a small fish tank lay smashed at the foot of a table. A number of small, tropical fish lay dead or dying, according to whether they had been catapulted high and dry or had managed to remain in the flow of water towards the door.

It required no more than a glance to see that the room had been ransacked. Everything lay scattered, including the bedclothing which was heaped on the floor.

Beneath a coarse, grey blanket a pair of legs stuck out. Clenching his teeth, Brian gingerly lifted the blanket and found himself staring into Harry Green's upturned face. His lifeless eyes stared back at Brian. One side of his head appeared to be a mass of blood.

Aghast, Brian dropped the blanket and ran out of the room.

His only thought was to get as far away as possible and he didn't stop running until he was clear of Hersholt Street.

It wasn't until he reached home that his mind began to function again.

CHAPTER NINE

Long before Brian arrived home, however, events in Hersholt Street were taking place. Indeed, they began when he had scarcely turned the corner in his flight from the scene.

The man who had been hovering in a doorway across the road from number 42 and who had witnessed both Brian's arrival and his departure slipped away from his hiding-place and hurried to the nearest public telephone which was in a neighbouring street.

He clucked indignantly when he found it occupied and moved a short distance off to keep it under observation. He didn't have to wait more than a minute before the woman inside left and he was able to make his call. With avid fingers he dialled 999 and asked for the police. When there was an answer, he said:

'You better send someone quick to forty-two Hersholt Street. I think something's 'appened there.'

'May I have your name, sir?' the voice at the other end asked in a politely neutral tone.

'Mr George Pratt.'

'Where are you speaking from, Mr Pratt?'

'From a call box just near to Hersholt Street.'

'And what is it that you think has happened at number forty-two?'

George Pratt bit at his lower lip in annoyance. He'd not expected an interrogation. On the contrary he'd believed police cars would be converging on Hersholt Street before he'd even had time to leave the phone box, their sirens sounding and their blue lights flashing.

'I think somebody may have got hurt,' he said. 'I see'd a young chap run out of the house just now and he 'ad a sort of wild look about him. 'E just ran and ran as if 'is life 'anged on it.'

'And what's your address, Mr Pratt?'

'What's my bloody address got to do wiv it? I thought you wanted the public to 'elp you catch criminals. That's what I'm doing and all I get is bloody questions.'

'Keep calm, Mr Pratt,' the voice said equably. 'Where'll you be when the police come?'

That was more like it, some action at last! 'I'll be hanging around near number forty-two,' Pratt said, mollified. 'I'll tell 'em what I know.'

The first car to arrive reached the house just as George Pratt was turning into the street. A young P.C. in uniform had got out and was staring up at the windows when Pratt came up to him.

'I'm Mr Pratt. I'm the one what's dialled nine, nine, nine.'

'Just hang on a moment here, sir, and we'll find out what's happened.'

With that the young officer pushed open the door and went in. Meanwhile the driver of the car who was still at the wheel unwound his window and leaned out, as though preparing to make a grab at Pratt should he suddenly take to his heels.

In less than a minute, however, the first officer emerged from the house. He looked shaken.

'There's a dead bloke upstairs in there, Ted,' he said to the driver.

'Better get on the blower.' Turning to Pratt, he added, 'You better wait in the car.' And he opened the rear door.

By the time he had walked round and got into the front passenger seat, the one called Ted had passed a terse message on the radio.

'I'm P.C. Best and this is P.C. Alington,' the first one said, swivelling round to look at George Pratt with undisguised interest. 'What do you know about this affair, Mr Pratt?'

'I saw this young chap run out of the 'ouse like I said on the phone,' Pratt said self-importantly. ''E 'ad a funny look about 'im, so that I naturally became suspicious and decided it was my duty to inform the police.'

'Do you think you'd recognise him again?'

'I'm good on faces so I reckon I might.'

'What sort of age was he?'

'Early twenties. Medium height. Longish 'air.'

'What was he wearing?'

''E was wearing a pair of darkish trousers and 'e 'ad on one of them anorak things which was zipped up at the front.'

While P.C. Best and Pratt had been talking, the driver had been conversing on the two-way radio with a disembodied voice which crackled as though powered by static electricity.

Another car now came to a swerving halt behind them and P.C. Best got out. Pratt saw him lead two plain clothes officers into the house.

A few minutes later a third, followed by a fourth, car arrived on the scene. By this time, too, a small crowd had gathered to watch events, exhibiting that bovine patience which characterises those who are drawn to the life and death dramas of every day.

It was half an hour before anyone paid further attention to George Pratt. Then one of the plain clothes officers came out of the house and got into the rear seat beside him.

'So you're the chap who raised the alarm?' he observed in a hearty bedside manner tone. 'George Pratt, isn't it?'

'Yes, I'm Mr Pratt.'

'Well, start at the beginning, Mr Pratt, and tell me everything you know.'

'I've already done that to your young colleague,' Pratt said stiffly.

'Forget about my young colleague and now tell me.'

'May I know who you are?' Pratt asked in a tone which was even stiffer.

'By all means. I'm Detective Sergeant Hanson of E division. Now start telling me!'

'As I've already explained, I saw this young feller dash out of the 'ouse and run off down the street. 'E was acting so suspicious, I decided it was my duty to inform the police, because I reckoned 'e might 'ave been up to no good.'

'Where were you when you saw him?'

'On the opposite side of the street.'

'Doing what?'

' 'Ow do you mean?'

'What were you doing on the opposite side of the street when you saw all this?'

'What was I doing?' Pratt echoed indignantly. 'I was walking along the pavement, of course. What else would I be doing?'

'Keep calm, Mr Pratt. You've been very helpful thus far and I'm sure you'll go on being so, but we have to find out everything we can, especially from an important witness like yourself, and the only way we can do that is by asking questions.'

'Of course,' Pratt replied, mollified once more.

'That's fine then. Tell me this: what was it in particular that aroused your suspicions?'

'The way 'e dashed out as if someone were after 'im. And 'e kept on looking back in a scared sort of way.'

Sergeant Hanson nodded thoughtfully.

'Do you happen to know who lives in number forty-two?'

''Course I don't! Never been inside the place!' His tone assumed its note of indignation again. 'Don't know anyone who lives in this street.'

'I was wondering about that. What exactly were you doing in this particular part of town?'

'I was meeting someone in that pub at the end of the street. The Plumbers Arms. But 'e never turned up.'

'What's the name of the friend you were due to meet?'

'I never said 'e was a friend. 'E was just a bloke I met last week and arranged to meet again this evening. I only knows 'im as Paddy.'

'So there's no need to ask where he comes from!' Sergeant Hanson remarked.

'But 'e never turned up.'

'So you said.'

'And that's 'ow I came to be passing by when this young feller dashed out.' A small note of triumph crept into George Pratt's tone as he rounded off his explanation.

'I understand that you think you might be able to recognise the chap if you were to see him again.'

'I reckon that's a possibility,' Pratt said complacently.

Sergeant Hanson was silent for a while. Then he said, 'Well, what we'll do now is go along to the station and get a written statement from you and then we'll have a car drive you home. O.K.?'

Pratt nodded. He reckoned he'd been pretty crafty.

He'd certainly scored points off this cocky C.I.D. sergeant.

'Just before we go, would you mind coming into the house and taking a look at the body?' Sergeant Hanson went on. 'It may be somebody you've seen before, in which case that'll help us.'

'I've told you I don't know who lives in that 'ouse.'

'That's right, but it may be someone you've come across at some time or another.'

Pratt threw Detective Sergeant Hanson a suspicious look. 'I don't see 'ow I can 'ave.'

'Anyway, are you willing to come in for a moment and see? It won't take more than a couple of minutes. Not that you have to if your mind's made up.'

'I don't like looking at bodies!'

'I'm with you, though one gets used to it in this job.'

'All right then, but I'm telling you now, it'll be a bloody waste of time.'

They got out of the car and Sergeant Hanson led the way into the house. The door of Harry Green's room was open and a photographer was standing on the threshold taking shots of the interior. Four plain clothes officers were bunched on the landing waiting for him to finish.

'This is Mr Pratt, sir,' Sergeant Hanson said to one of them who resembled a retired heavyweight boxer. Turning to Pratt, he added, 'Detective Inspector Gilroy is in charge of the case.'

Gilroy grunted. 'Only until the next man up arrives.' He glanced at George Pratt without favour. 'Knows the dead man, does he?' he asked, turning back to Sergeant Hanson.

'Volunteered to see if he did,' Sergeant Hanson replied smoothly, while Pratt scowled.

'Let him get on with it then. And mind he doesn't tread on any of the blasted fish. Don't want them turned into fish paste before the scene of crime officer gets here.'

Sergeant Hanson steered Pratt just inside the room and pointed at Harry Green's corpse.

Pratt gave a shudder and shook his head vigorously. 'Never seen 'im in my life before, so 'elp me God!'

Sergeant Hanson, who had been observing him closely, motioned him to leave.

They were about to go back downstairs when Detective Inspector Gilroy spoke. 'Just a moment, Sergeant, before you leave.' Glancing towards Pratt, he added, 'He'll be with you in a minute. Go and wait in the car, will you.' Then turning back to Hanson, he said, 'What the hell was that all in aid of, bringing him up to look at the body?'

'There's something odd about his whole story, sir. I thought it'd be useful to see how he reacted.'

'And was it?' Gilroy asked with an edge to his tone.

'Not really.'

There was a short silence while Gilroy stared at his sergeant as though trying to decide whether to have him boiled or roasted. Finally, he said in a grating voice, 'As far as I'm concerned, Mr bloody Pratt is an important witness—our one and only witness at the moment—and I don't want him frightened off by someone's clever tricks. God knows, we get few enough members of the public coming forward to help us at any bloody time, so we don't want to scare away the few who do. Do we, Sergeant?'

'No, sir.'

'Right, well get on with it then!'

As Sergeant Hanson shot off downstairs, Gilroy muttered darkly, 'It seems as if young detective sergeants regard murder enquiries as bloody initiative tests these days.'

Sergeant Hanson didn't put his own thoughts into words, not even muttered ones, but he reminded himself that he wasn't surprised the police had a recruiting problem when officers like Detective Inspector Gilroy ruled the local roosts.

To make matters worse, it was clear from George Pratt's demeanour that he sensed Sergeant Hanson had, as he saw it, been further cut down to size. Consequently, the drive to the police station was accomplished in silence. Pratt sat back in his corner of the car feeling well satisfied with himself while Detective Sergeant Hanson continued to smart in his.

As their car moved away from the kerb, its place was taken by one bringing the Detective Chief Superintendent of the division to the scene of the crime. It was the first evening in three weeks that he'd arrived home as early as seven o'clock and, though his wife had been pleased to see him, each of them had felt it was too good to last. Thus, the telephone call shortly before nine o'clock had been received with resignation and no surprise. It had happened too often before.

Detective Chief Superintendent Chivers had been appointed to his present post only three months previously. With the appointment had come promotion. In age he was about half-way between Detective Sergeant Hanson and Detective Inspector Gilroy. His views on the D.I. were not much different from Sergeant Hanson's.

On arriving upstairs at number 42, he stood for a while in the doorway of Harry Green's room just surveying the scene and trying to impress as much of its detail as he could on his mind. He always remembered a wise old detective telling him, after he'd first joined the C.I.D., to use his eyes before his tongue. It was advice he'd neither forgotten nor ever regretted.

Detective Inspector Gilroy watched him stonily and spoke when he considered what was to him an affectation anyway had lasted long enough.

'Cause of death, blows to the head by that hammer,' he said nodding in the direction of the hammer which lay on the floor close to the body. 'We're waiting for the pathologist, but the divisional surgeon has been and confirmed that was the probable cause of death. Not that it really needed a doctor to tell us.'

'Several blows by the look of it,' Chivers observed, bending down to inspect the head.

'At least three, I'd say.'

'Which pathologist is coming?'

'Professor Paxford. He should be here any moment.'

Chivers straightened up and let his gaze continue round the room.

'Somebody's made a right mess of the place. Wonder what they were looking for?'

Gilroy shrugged. 'We'll probably know that when we know a bit more about the deceased.'

'Who is he?'

'Name of Harry Green.' Inspector Gilroy stared at the upturned face. 'Looks like a C.R.O. type to me.'

Chivers nodded. He had drawn the same conclusion himself. 'No one else in the house?'

'No. I've had someone enquire at the neighbours'. Seems the house is rented by a Mrs Green who is away. Nobody seems to know where exactly, save that it's thought she's staying with a married daughter somewhere in Yorkshire. She's believed to be the deceased's sister-in-law. He's only been lodging here a few weeks, so the woman next door says.'

'Did any of them hear anything? There must have been quite a noise up here.'

'Nobody heard a thing! And you know why?'

'They were watching T.V., which was turned on full blast.'

Gilroy nodded sourly. He hadn't intended his question to be answered with such matter-of-factness.

'Does that mean we're starting from cold? No witnesses or anything?'

'On the contrary, we have a very important witness. He's at the station now, giving a statement to Detective

71

Sergeant Hanson,' Gilroy said and went on to give Chivers the gist of George Pratt's evidence.

'We should be able to build up an identikit picture from the description he gives us,' Chivers said hopefully.

Gilroy grunted contemptuously. 'If you ask me, all identikit pictures look exactly like the same character out of a strip cartoon.'

'May still be better than nothing.' Chivers gave the room another panning look. 'Any fingerprints?'

'A few smudgy ones, but they'll probably turn out to be the deceased's. The hammer hasn't been properly examined yet. It may reveal some.'

'Either the fish tank got overturned in a struggle or the deceased knocked it over as he fell,' Chivers remarked thoughtfully.

'Don't see that it much matters which way it happened!'

Chivers didn't agree but refrained from saying so.

At this moment, Professor Paxford arrived in the room.

'Good evening, Chief Superintendent, good evening, Inspector,' he murmured as he bent down beside the corpse, his glance darting around as he did so.

Slipping on a pair of rubber gloves, he examined Harry Green's head as if it might have been a prize-winning peach.

'Been dead between two and three hours. Am I right?'

'Probably died sometime around eight o'clock,' Gilroy said.

'That makes it nearer two than three. Always difficult to tell exactly. It's only in books that the time of death is tied to seconds.' He grinned disarmingly. 'In many cases, I'd never get it within hours if the police couldn't give me a few clues.' He stood up. 'All right, Chief Superintendent, get the body to the mortuary as soon as you like and I'll get on with the p.m. You certainly don't need me to tell you that you've got a case of murder on your hands.'

CHAPTER TEN

Of the two members of Fiona's lot he had met, Brian had taken least fancy to Roscoe. Not that he regarded either of them as congenial. Roscoe had shoulder length hair which he wore parted in the middle. His beard looked as though it could do with a good application of fertiliser and finally there were his spectacles, circular and steel-rimmed which perched on his high-bridged nose as though awaiting the moment to spring at someone.

Accordingly, the last person whom Brian wished to see when he arrived home at the end of his flight from the scene of Harry Green's death was Roscoe. Nevertheless, it was Roscoe who was sitting cross-legged on the floor of their room talking to Fiona who was reclining on the bed like a beached seal.

'Hello, love,' she said, jumping up and throwing her arms round his neck.

'Hello, mate,' Roscoe said in a tone devoid of any personal warmth.

Fiona kissed him while Roscoe watched them with an expression of detached superiority.

'Why don't we all go out and have a pizza at Mario's?' Fiona said eagerly.

Brian shook his head. 'You and Roscoe go if you want. I'll stay here.'

Fiona's expression became immediately anxious. 'Is something the matter, love? You look worried.'

'You go out if you want. I'll be here when you get back.'

Brian avoided looking at Roscoe, aware that he was being subjected to cold scrutiny.

'Well, I shan't go if you're not coming, love.'

A short, uncomfortable silence fell which was eventually broken by Roscoe rising up off the floor as though hoisted on a wire. 'O.K., Fiona, I'll shit off,' he said in a bored tone. 'Make nice love!'

As soon as the door was closed behind him, Fiona turned to Brian.

'Tell me what's happened, love,' she said gently, pulling him down on the bed beside her and cradling his head in her lap.

When he had finished, she was silent for a minute. Then she said, 'That's all right, love. You haven't got anything to worry about. The only two living people who know you went to the house are you and me.'

'But supposing Harry Green told someone before he was killed.'

'Doesn't make sense. He obviously wanted to see you on some personal matter, in which case he'd have kept his arrangements to himself.'

'Do you really think that?'

She nodded eagerly. 'Yes, I do. Nobody in the whole world outside of this room need ever know that you went to forty-two Hersholt Street this evening.' She paused. 'I wonder who did kill the poor sod! Probably someone who knew he had money stashed away in his room.'

'It certainly looked as though every corner had been searched.'

'Then that's pretty certain what happened. Somebody's doing a spot of burglary when Green returns home and the burglar cracks him over the head.'

'There'd been a struggle, too.'

'Doesn't alter the general picture.' She bent down and kissed the tip of his chin. 'Feeling better, now?'

'In a way, but I still wish I knew a bit more of what's gone on.'

'It's probably as well you don't. You've played your small part, been paid off and now you're out of the show altogether. The less you know, the better. Just keep your mouth shut and you're untouchable. Except by me,' she added with a giggle, giving him a long kiss to which he responded with a sudden feeling of relief and confidence; relief that Fiona had allayed the worst of his anxiety and confidence that she was right in her predictions.

'What about just you and me going along to Mario's?' she said, running her fingers through his hair.

'You don't think we'll run into Roscoe?'

'Do you mind if we do?'

'I wouldn't mind if we didn't.'

She laughed. 'Roscoe's all right, when you know him.'

'What was he doing here this evening?'

'We were just discussing various things. Incidentally, he likes you.'

'He may pretend to for your sake.'

'No, he's said so.'

'He gives me the creeps.'

'That's an unfair, subjective judgment.'

'You know I don't understand you when you talk like that. What the hell's a subjective judgment? Anyway, I don't want to know. Let's be gone to Mario's.'

When they returned, they were both pleasantly sleepy. In thirty seconds dead, they had each thrown off their clothes and got into bed. Brian's last memory before falling asleep was of Fiona curling a soft arm around his midriff.

When he awoke the next morning, the feeling of foreboding was with him again, but then, as he lay cocooned in the warmth of their bed, it began to lift. He recalled the arguments which Fiona had advanced the previous evening and they again seemed persuasive. He glanced at

her sleeping presence beside him, grateful in an inde-
finable way for the strength she brought to the relationship. The strength she gave him. There'd never been
anyone else in his life before who had done this.

It was with reluctance that he eventually got up and
dressed. She was still asleep when he'd drunk a cup of
coffee and was ready to leave. She never did get up till
midday and madly as she professed to be in love with
him, her devotion seldom extended to sharing this part
of the day with him.

It was ten o'clock when Brian left the house to walk
to the underground station. The rush-hour traffic was over
and the pavements, having rid themselves of scurrying
office workers, were occupied with the more leisurely pro-
gress of mothers with prams and push-chairs making for
the shops.

At the station Brian bought a paper, but didn't open
it until he was in the train. When he did so, his heart
gave a jump as he saw a short paragraph headed, 'London
man found murdered'.

He quickly raised the paper so as to hide his face from
fellow passengers. The piece read:

'Following a 999 call, police went last night to 42 Hersholt Street, N.W.1. where they found the dead body of
a man, believed to be Mr Harry Green, aged 46, of the
same address. Mr Green appeared to have died as a
result of head injuries. The police wish to interview a
young man aged between 20 and 23 and of medium
height who was seen leaving the house shortly after a
quarter past eight yesterday evening.'

For what seemed an eternity, Brian held the paper in
front of his face while his mind reeled from the shock of
what he'd just read. He half-expected when he lowered it
to find the carriage full of policemen all staring in his

direction. In the event, a decision was made for him when the newspaper was swept from his hands by a fat woman's shopping bag as she moved to get out.

He glanced furtively about him, ready to make a dash for it before the doors closed if danger seemed imminent. But no one was paying him any attention save for the girl opposite who had picked up his paper and was offering it to him with a pleasant smile. He nodded his thanks and spent the next few minutes folding it with exaggerated care in an endeavour to occupy his hands and keep them from trembling. It was either that or sitting on them.

The girl got out at the next station and for the remainder of his journey, Brian stared grimly out of the window as he tried to reassemble his thoughts from their state of disarray. Eventually he felt able to take another look at the paper. This time he managed to read the item without any untoward display of emotion.

After all, what did it amount to, other than someone had seen him leaving the house! Whoever it was couldn't have got much of a view of him, hence the vague description. There must be at least a million people who answered to that! So what was he worrying about! Of course, it had come as a nasty shock seeing he'd no idea that anyone had seen him leave, but, now that the initial sense of shock was receding, he began to feel more secure again.

He got out at Holborn Station as usual, but, instead of making his way straight to the Blackstone, he bought another paper and went into a nearby café to read it. It carried a piece similar to that in the first paper, except that it didn't mention Harry Green's name and referred to the person whom the police wished to interview simply as 'a young man', without any further description.

Brian discarded the paper and left the café. When he got to the club, he'd find an opportunity of looking through all the other papers. The Blackstone took the lot, though he seldom saw members reading any other than *The Times* and *The Daily Telegraph*. Anyway he'd glance through them before the club opened at noon, not that he expected to find anything more detailed than what he'd already read.

Talbot was the first person he saw when he arrived. The old wine steward was examining his chin in the yellowing mirror which was a fixture on the wall of the back passage, in particular a pustular spot on the side of his chin.

'It's all that dreadful man's doing, bringing me out in spots,' he said indignantly. 'I hadn't had any since I was a boy until he started getting me upset. Incidentally, he's here now. Upstairs with the secretary.'

'Any news on the burglary?'

'No. And if you ask me there never will be. I was speaking to Sir Anthony Charles last night. He's the famous Q.C. I don't suppose you know him yet as he hasn't been in the club for some time. He's always abroad on big cases and he's only just back from Hong Kong. But he says it'll be a fluke if the police ever manage to catch the men who did it. He thought it was disgraceful the way I'd been treated by that man. He says it's no wonder the police don't get the co-operation from the public these days when they don't know how to behave like gentlemen.'

Brian had listened to this denunciation while waiting for it only to end. As soon as Talbot resumed the examination of his complexion in the mirror, he hurried off.

It was always one of his first duties of a morning to go round the smoking-room and make sure there were no glasses left there from the previous evening and also see that the cleaner had emptied all the ash trays.

Having done this, he normally returned to the wine pantry to do any odd jobs of preparation that remained, failing which he'd go into the kitchen for a cup of coffee and a gossip.

On this occasion, however, he went over to the table where the newspapers were laid out and began working his way through them. Such was his absorption that he didn't hear the smoking-room door open.

'Now, look what a mess you've made of those papers!' Talbot said testily. 'Anyway, what are you doing reading them? You'd better go, I'll tidy them up. You should know that Judge Whitby-Stansford expects to find them untouched when he arrives.' Talbot began fussing with the paper which Brian had just put down. 'Well, get along, he's waiting for you,' he said.

'Who?'

'That policeman. He wants to speak to you. He's up in the secretary's room.'

'You never said he wanted to see me,' Brian said suspiciously.

'What are you talking about! I've come specially looking for you to tell you. The secretary phoned down.' He gave a censorious cluck. 'This *Daily Telegraph* looks as if you've been wrapping yourself up in it! I don't know what the members will think.'

Brian left the room, his mind once more that morning in turmoil. As he mounted the stairs, he kept impressing on himself that he must play it cool. He mustn't let them see how rattled he felt. He must be ready for anything.

The 'come-in' which followed his knock on the door sounded reassuringly friendly. Sitting at the secretary's desk was Detective Chief Superintendent Samson and over in a corner of the room was Detective Sergeant Ellis.

'Come in and sit down, Tanner,' Samson said affably, while Sergeant Ellis gave him a wink.

Brian sat forward on the edge of a chair and waited. It didn't seem as though they were about to produce the hand-cuffs, but he mustn't allow himself to become lulled into a false sense of security. He knew from experience that the police were never more dangerous than when they were being nice to you.

'I thought I'd like to have a word with you myself about the burglary,' Samson went on. 'It may be that you can help where others can't.'

Brian cocked his head to one side like a robin. What were they getting at?

'You've been working here for about three months, is that right?'

'Yes.'

'And you look a fairly bright, intelligent sort of young man! Think hard before you answer this, but have you ever noticed anyone showing particular interest in the show cases where the snuff-boxes were kept?'

Brian frowned. Whatever he'd expected, it wasn't to be tapped as a possible informant.

'I suppose,' he said hesitantly, 'that Judge Whitby-Stansford used to.' He noticed Detective Sergeant Ellis make a quick note in the pocketbook which was balanced on his knee. 'I don't think anyone else really did, sir, except when they had guests. Members were always showing them to their guests, but they didn't seem to give them a lot of notice otherwise.'

'Apart from Judge Whitby-Stansford?'

'Yes, one often saw him looking at them by himself. But I'm sure it was only because he was interested in those sort of things.'

'Of course,' Samson observed dryly.

'I mean, I don't want you to think I'm suggesting...'

Samson held up a deprecating hand. 'You've been very helpful. It's precisely what I wanted to get from you. Impressions. You needn't fear that we're going to rush off and arrest anyone on the strength of what you tell us within these four walls. It's all a question of trying to piece together a background.' He picked up a packet of cigarettes from the desk and offered one to Brian, following it up with a light. 'Now, let's see if you can help on something else,' he continued, fixing Brian with a sudden searchlight look. 'What's your view of old Talbot? Do you think he's capable of having arranged this burglary?'

'I'm sure he couldn't have,' Brian said with a vehemence which Samson hadn't expected.

'You like him, do you?'

Brian shrugged. 'Not especially.'

'And yet you leap to his defence! You see, I can understand the secretary and Mr Justice Pearn and all that lot standing up for him. He's been with the club for over forty years and to them it's unthinkable that he might have had any part in the burglary. He's the faithful club servant personified. Rather he drop dead than that the Blackstone should suffer any damage. I've been hearing it on all sides ever since I set foot inside this place. But compared with the others, you're an outsider, Tanner. I hoped you'd give me a less biassed view.' He sighed. 'Anyway, why don't you think he could have had anything to do with it? Let's see if we can analyse Talbot's apparent magic spells. Because that's what it seems like. Suspect Talbot and it seems you're sinning against the Holy Ghost. Now, I can't really believe you feel that, so why are you so sure he's in the clear?'

'Because, why should he suddenly do this after forty years here?'

It was Samson's turn to shrug. 'Because it's happened before,' he said wearily. 'Not with Talbot, I don't mean, but with the likes of him. Faithful servants suddenly bite the hand that's been feeding them all the years. Usually, because it suddenly dawns on them just how badly they've been fed! Ever heard Talbot complain about his treatment here?'

'No.'

81

'Know anything about his friends or contacts?'

'Nothing.'

'Has he said anything to you since the burglary?'

'About it?'

'Yes.'

'Nothing to suggest he had anything to do with it. He's very upset that he's come under suspicion.'

'So I keep on being told! But it doesn't help to remove the suspicion.' He gave Brian an almost imploring look. 'Wouldn't you suspect him if you were in my place?'

'I suppose I should.'

'Well, let's just squeeze this lemon finally dry! Even though you profess to have no particular liking for Talbot, you're convinced he had nothing to do with the burglary?'

'That's right.'

'I wonder why! I wonder why!' Samson observed in an abstracted tone, which caused Brian to fidget in an embarrassed way. After a short silence, he glanced up from the desk which had been absorbing his concentrated thoughts. 'That'll be all for the moment, Tanner. You haven't helped me as much as I hoped you might, but it hasn't been a complete waste of time.'

Brian got up and looked from one officer to the other, but neither was paying him any attention.

As he went back downstairs, he couldn't help being amused by the irony of the situation. That he should have been selected for this particular approach. It amused him, too, that he had been able to tell them the truth about Talbot. He didn't like him, that was absolutely true. And he *was* convinced the old wine steward had nothing to do with the burglary, that was also true.

A sudden frown furrowed his brow. He was basing his judgment on the fact that Talbot had had no part in the act of burglary itself, but did this necessarily exclude him from every other role? After all, he could have

82

planned the whole thing. But if he'd done that, he'd have made sure that suspicion couldn't fall on him in the way it had.

By the time he reached the bottom stair, Brian's faith in Talbot's innocence was restored. Whoever *was* behind the burglary, it couldn't be him. This feeling was reinforced when he reached the wine pantry where Talbot was polishing glasses.

For a while, each of them worked in silence, Talbot tight-lipped and frowning in an obviously determined effort not to be the first to broach the subject which was uppermost in both their minds. Eventually, however, he was unable to bear the strain any longer.

'Well?' he said, giving Brian a resentful look. 'What did he want to know?'

'Er ... er, nothing in particular. He just wondered if I had any ideas as to who might have had anything to do with it.'

Talbot's frown increased. 'He has no right talking to junior staff in such a way. You should report what he said to the secretary. I hope you remembered to hold your tongue.'

Brian turned away. He was damned if he was going to be spoken to like that, particularly after he'd stuck up for the old sod. O.K., let him sweat a bit! He was aware that Talbot wanted to ask him further questions from the fact that he kept on finding additional reasons for remaining in the wine pantry. In the end, he began polishing a tray of glasses for the second time. Brian, however, appeared to ignore him and went about his own duties.

When the silence had become almost palpable and Talbot was showing signs of explosive nervous suppression, Brian made to leave the pantry himself.

'By the way,' Talbot said in a taut voice as Brian reached the door, 'did he mention me?'

Brian assumed a mystified expression.

'I'm sorry?'

'Did that man ask you about me?'

'The policeman you mean?' Talbot nodded grimly. 'Yes, your name did come up.'

'What did he ask you about me?'

'Only how long I'd known you and that sort of thing.'

Talbot pursed his lips, torn between vital curiosity and the desire not to appear to be pumping his assistant for information, behaviour which he regarded as demeaning.

'I hope you were properly discreet,' he said loftily. 'Not that I have anything to worry about. Sir John and others have assured me of that. But we have to remember the Blackstone's reputation in all this.'

With this parting shot, he squeezed past Brian and set off in the direction of the dining-room.

Pompous old fool, Brian reflected. Doesn't even know who his friends are. Serve him right if he does have his tail twisted further by the police. Why should I bother to help him!

By the time the club opened its doors at noon that day, the police had departed and, apart from the empty display cases as a reminder of what had happened, life within the Blackstone's walls had resumed its leisured appearance. Though members in the dining-room still enquired casually of their neighbours whether there was any further news about the burglary, it had ceased to be the number one topic of conversation and it certainly failed to keep awake those, like ex-Judge Whitby-Stansford, who, after lunch, took their customary siesta in the smoking-room. Brian was on duty the whole afternoon which meant a slack hour or two between clearing up after lunch and waiting for the sleepers to awake. By three o'clock, the club was always virtually deserted, even the late lunchers having departed by then, in addition to a lot of the part-time staff who only came in to help at mealtimes.

Brian usually spent this period, sitting in a corner of

the kitchen reading his favourite author, Mickey Spillane. Talbot always retired to his own room at the top of the building and lay down for a couple of hours. He had long reached the position when he was excused afternoon duty.

About four o'clock, the bell summoned Brian to the smoking-room. One of them must have woken early today, he thought to himself as he made his way there.

When he arrived it was to find ex-Judge Whitby-Stansford in his usual chair and in sole occupation.

'Bring me some tea and a toasted bun,' the old man said, gazing at him through bleary eyes.

Five minutes later, Brian returned with the order and put the tray down on the table beside his chair.

Ex-Judge Whitby-Stansford pulled out the purse in which he carried his money and handed Brian a coin.

'What's your name?' he asked, suddenly.

'Brian, sir.'

'Brian. Is that what you're called here?'

'Yes.'

'What's your other name?'

'Tanner, sir.'

'Like it here, do you, Tanner?'

'It's all right, sir.'

'All right! Young fellows like you have got no feeling for tradition, have you?'

'I can't say, sir.'

'You heed tradition, Tanner, it's what this country's founded on. And a fine thing, too! Too much being destroyed these days and nothing worthwhile being put in its place.'

Brian listened impassively, wondering what had suddenly caused the old boy to give tongue. Ex-Judge Whitby-Stansford bit into his bun and Brian watched a trickle of melted butter descend his chin.

'Look at this burglary we've just had,' the old man went on. 'Couldn't have happened thirty years ago. Now, nothing's sacred, even if some of the items were a lot of rubbish!'

'I can see it was a blow for the club, sir,' Brian felt compelled to say under pressure of the stare ex-Judge Whitby-Stansford was directing at him.

'A blow! Is that what you call it, Tanner? It was a scandal.'

'In what way do you mean, sir?'

'A scandal that the club allowed it to happen. Serves them right in some ways!'

'Them, sir?'

'The committee. Wouldn't listen to advice!'

Though Brian waited, ex-Judge Whitby-Stansford said nothing more. Indeed, the next time he looked up at Brian, it was as though he was seeing him for the first time.

'I've paid you, haven't I?' he asked, faintly querulously.

'Yes, sir.'

'Fetch me *Punch* before you go.'

Brian went over to the table where the magazines were set out, but failed to find what he was looking for.

'I'm afraid it doesn't seem to be here, sir.'

'Then bring me the complaints book!'

It had been a curious conversation, Brian reflected, as he returned to the kitchen. Perhaps the old boy was going a bit round the bend. He'd heard how old men did have strange turns and talk a bit odd, especially, now he came to think of it, just after they'd woken up. Perhaps that was the explanation.

When he returned to the smoking-room to take the ex-judge a large pink gin about two hours later, there was no further conversation, though his name was still recalled.

'Tell the porter to get me a taxi in about twenty minutes' time, will you, Tanner?'

'It's not my flaming job to find him taxis,' the porter grumbled when Brian conveyed this message. At that moment, one drew up at the door to discharge a passenger and the porter hopped outside. 'You can go and tell him the meter's ticking up nicely,' he said when he came back in.

'You go and tell him,' Brian said and walked off. He didn't like the porter, anyway.

The next day passed uneventfully with Harry Green's murder not even further mentioned in any of the papers. In an age of violence, his death was not a particularly newsworthy occurrence, for which Brian was grateful. Having it plastered all over the papers would have made him feel distinctly uncomfortable. As it was, he was able to persuade himself that, midst more important crimes, it probably wouldn't have a very high place on the list of police priorities.

He was able to delude himself, that is, until he arrived home around half past eight that evening. Fiona had told him she'd be out and he was pondering what he was going to do as he climbed the stairs to their room. He had just inserted the key in the lock when he was suddenly aware of movement on either side of him.

'Mind if we come in for a chat?' Detective Sergeant Hanson said.

Brian turned his head sharply to look at the person on his other side and received a wink from Detective Sergeant Ellis.

CHAPTER ELEVEN

Brian had been so taken by surprise that the hand which had been about to open the door fell to his side as though paralysed and it was Detective Sergeant Hanson who, in fact, turned the key.

Inside the room, the two officers glanced about them with the curiosity of a couple of cats while Brian stood watching them in a state of numbed apprehension.

'I believe you know Detective Sergeant Ellis?' Sergeant Hanson said, standing on tiptoe in an effort to see what was on top of the cupboard. 'I'm Detective Sergeant Hanson of E division and I'm concerned in enquiries into the murder of one Harry Green.' As he mentioned the dead man's name, he swung round to face Brian.

Brian hoped his expression did nothing to reveal the state of his mind.

'Heard of him?' Sergeant Hanson enquired in the same conversational tone.

'No, I don't think I know anyone of that name.'

'Well, you can't know him now because he's dead; but what I asked was, have you ever heard of anyone of that name?'

'No, not that I recall.'

'You don't seem too sure.'

'Well, it's a fairly ordinary sort of name, isn't it!' Brian remarked with a show of spirit which both surprised and encouraged him.

'Would you say it was an ordinary sort of name, Sergeant?' Hanson said, turning to Sergeant Ellis.

Ellis appeared to ponder the question. 'I'd certainly remember if I'd ever met anyone of that name,' he replied with an air of judicial gravity.

'Just so. But apparently not our young friend here. He's unable to recall whether he ever knew a Harry Green or not.' He fixed his gaze on Brian again. 'But perhaps you can remember better now you've had an opportunity of thinking?'

Brian shook his head. 'No, I definitely don't know anyone of that name.'

Sergeant Hanson sighed, as though Brian had moved a piece in a chess game which merely postponed an inevitable check mate.

'So this is where you live with your girl-friend?' Sergeant Ellis said, studying a poster picture of Che Guevara on the wall. 'Where's she at the moment?'

'Out.'

'You could have fooled me! I thought she was under the bed.' He shook his head reproachfully. 'Where out?'

'I don't know.'

'When'll she be back?'

'About midnight.'

'What does she do?'

'She's a social worker.'

'A do-gooder, is she!'

All the time, the two men continued to survey their surroundings like cats in a new home.

It was Sergeant Hanson who spoke next. 'So if you've never heard of Harry Green, I suppose you've never heard of Hersholt Street either?'

Brian passed his tongue across his lips which had become uncomfortably dry. He could always squirm out of his last lie by saying, if necessary, that he'd known Harry Green by a different name, but it wouldn't be open to him to do this if he now denied having heard of Hersholt Street.

'I think I have,' he said, frowning as though trying to recall a specific occasion.

'He thinks he has,' Sergeant Hanson commented. 'O.K., when were you last in Hersholt Street?'

'I didn't say I'd ever been there, only that I thought I'd heard of it.'

'Crafty, isn't he?' Hanson observed to the room at large. 'Some might say a bit too crafty, a bit too devious. Almost gives the impression of not wanting to answer questions frankly. Don't you agree, Sergeant?'

'Yes, I do and it's not what I'd have expected from my little chat with him the other day at the Blackstone Club.'

Brian found he was grateful for these small rallies of sarcastic by-play between the two officers as they afforded him an opportunity of trying to work out what must have happened to bring the two of them to where he lived. The one fact which stuck out with ominous clarity was that Harry Green's death and the theft of the snuff-boxes had become linked and this was highly disagreeable in its implications. Brian felt his predicament to be that of someone suddenly blindfolded and pushed into a strange room. One false step could prove disastrous. Moreover, he couldn't be sure that he hadn't already made the first.

'Any objection if we search this room?' Sergeant Hanson asked, peering behind the cupboard.

'Why should you?' Brian replied. If he was going to be cornered, he'd turn and fight. 'You haven't got a search warrant.'

'Well, well, just harken to that!' Hanson said, his eyebrows raised in an expression of mock concern.

'I doubt whether we need a warrant,' Sergeant Ellis remarked. 'After all, he invited us in.'

'That's right, he did invite us in, didn't he! But of course if he wants to make difficulties, I can easily go off and get a warrant while you stay here.'

Ellis nodded. 'He probably doesn't know one can apply to a magistrate for a search warrant at any hour of the day or night.' He turned towards Brian. 'All Sergeant Hanson has to do is to go along to the nearest magistrate's home and apply for a search warrant under the Theft Act saying that he believes valuable snuff-boxes are hidden at this address.'

Brian tried hard not to look relieved. He knew from his previous brushes with the law that the one thing to avoid was teasing the police. They didn't like it and they were liable to over-react if they thought you were being uppish with them. You might be able to get away with it if you were a citizen of some standing, but if you were just Brian Tanner, you didn't stand a chance. He'd already sailed close to the wind once or twice this evening, so he had better watch his step from now on.

He gave a resigned shrug. 'All right, you can search the room if you want.'

Sergeant Hanson gave a satisfied nod. 'It's never too late to be sensible.'

Brian watched him as he went across to the cupboard and pulled open the door. He wasn't many years older than Brian himself and had a pleasant face. If you'd met him in the pub, you wouldn't have taken him for a C.I.D. officer. He even had quite long hair. But it just showed, Brian reflected, what a touch of authority did for some people. Give them the opportunity and they were flexing their power muscles like dolphins.

His gaze went to Sergeant Ellis who was older by a few years and who had somehow given the impression of being less enthusiastic than his colleague. It was as if he had supported him only in order to give the necessary appearance of solidarity.

While Hanson continued his examination of the cupboard, Ellis pulled the bed out from the wall and peered all round it.

Standing against the door, Brian watched them work their way methodically around the room. Ellis finished first and sat down on the bed. Hanson, however, began examining the floor, pulling back the linoleum where it touched the wall to see if any floorboards had recently been disturbed. Brian's apprehension returned and his mind raced to think of an explanation for his possession of the money should it be discovered.

'How long's this been here?' Hanson asked, tapping a sheet of asbestos behind the gas ring.

'It was here when we came.'

'Ever been removed?'

Brian shook his head, unable to trust his voice.

'It's loose,' Hanson remarked.

'I hadn't noticed.'

After that it was simply a matter of counting seconds as Sergeant Hanson wrenched the sheet away from the wall to reveal a onetime fireplace.

The metal grate was still in place and resting in it was an air travel bag. With a look of greedy triumph, Hanson seized the bag and swung it aloft.

Brian held his breath and waited. At moments of tension, the mind seems to take refuge in strange matter-of-factness, so that all he could think was, 'If he's expecting to find snuff-boxes in there, he's got a shock coming!'

And so it turned out to be as Sergeant Hanson eagerly unzipped the bag, only to let out a surprised whistle.

'Take a look at this,' he said to Ellis. 'Stacks of fivers.' Then glancing up at Brian, he asked, 'This your money?'

'Yes.'

'How much is there?'

'About seven hundred quid.'

'Care to tell us where you got it from?'

'It's my savings.'

'Your savings!'

'Yes.'

Though he hardly expected them to believe him, he had decided that it would be the safest answer in so far as it couldn't be so readily disproved as others. His first thought had been to say he'd won it gambling or been given it, but both of these would have led to further questions of when and where, which would ultimately have revealed them as lies.

Sergeant Hanson appeared thoughtful for a moment.

'I'm taking possession of this little lot,' he said, reaching what appeared to be a sudden decision. 'I'll give you a receipt and you'll get it all back. Provided it doesn't turn out to be the proceeds of crime!'

Brian watched him re-zip the bag, before whispering something in Sergeant Ellis' ear.

'Got a sheet of paper?' he asked.

Brian opened a drawer and handed him a pad of cheap writing-paper which belonged to Fiona. Hanson wrote out a receipt and handed it to him.

'We'll want to see you again soon, so don't go away,' he said, as he passed through the door on his way out.

When it came, their departure was almost as abrupt as their original appearance. For several seconds after they'd gone, Brian stood and stared at the now empty cavity behind the gas ring.

Something didn't quite fit with what had just happened and his mind groped to identify what was scratching beneath its surface.

Then suddenly realisation came. They had given him a receipt for the money without even counting it. After doubting everything else he'd told them, they had apparently taken his word for that.

CHAPTER TWELVE

As usual their meeting promised to break up long before it actually happened. The trouble was, as Fiona had the insight to recognise, each of them talked too much and listened too little. On this particular evening, however, she wanted to get away quickly as an intuitive sense told her that something had happened to Brian. But as she knew that the others were not too happy about her involvement with him she didn't wish to make him the excuse for her departure. Lately, she found herself increasingly on the defensive whenever his name came up in discussion.

The room in which they met was thick with cigarette smoke and the floor littered with butts. It was as sparsely furnished as a prison cell and rather less comfortable.

Over in a corner were two ancient mattresses with a tangle of blankets at one end. This was the communal bed. The room's advantage as a meeting-place lay in the fact that the occupants of the house were wholly incurious about each other's business. In turn, the outside world was incurious about them. The property was scheduled for demolition and, until the squad arrived to raze it, the less the local authorities had to know about it the happier they were.

Fiona was sitting on the mattress waiting to choose a moment to slip away when Hive came back into the room carrying two chipped mugs of black coffee. He walked over to where she was and handed her one of the mugs.

She gave him a fleeting smile and he squatted down on his haunches opposite her.

'You've been quiet of late,' he said, fixing her with his melancholy gaze. 'Want to say what's wrong?'

'Nothing's wrong, Hive.'

'It's Tanner, isn't it? You've got him bad.' Fiona stared back at him as though hypnotised by his voice. 'I should have stepped in before,' he went on unemotionally. 'It's my fault for letting it get to this stage. He just doesn't belong with us. You belong with us, Fiona, but you don't belong with him. I think it's time you broke with him. At this juncture of our affairs, it's dangerous to continue with him.'

'I can't. He needs me.' Her voice was small and flat.

'It was a mistake my letting you take up with him,' Hive went on as though she hadn't spoken. 'Roscoe agrees.'

'And Arthur?'

'Yes, Arthur, too. And you agree, as well, Fiona, if you're honest. You must leave him, otherwise he'll destroy you. You'll soon forget him. We'll help you to.' He put out a hand and gently touched her cheek, as if giving her some sort of blessing.

'But he's been helping us,' Fiona said in a pleading voice.

'That was also a mistake. We can do without his help. It's dangerous to accept help from outsiders. We all know that.'

'But he's not an outsider!'

'He is, Fiona. And he's slowly drawing you away from us.'

'That's not true,' she exclaimed. 'I don't know why you're suddenly talking like this.'

'It's for your own good! Our good!' He stretched out his arms and gripped her shoulders. His voice was fierce as he went on, 'Are you going to throw everything away for a few nights of sex? Are you going to let everyone down for that?'

'I can't let Brian down either.'

'It's better to dedicate yourself to a hundred thousand Brians than just a particular one. It's causes that count, not individuals.'

Fiona shivered. She had known that such a showdown must come, but she had hoped it might be indefinitely postponed. At this moment all she knew was that she must get back to Brian as soon as possible.

'I must have time to think,' she said, brushing Hive's hands from her shoulders and getting up.

He rose to his feet as well. 'Yes, but not too much time,' he said, turning away.

Brian was lying on the bed staring at the ceiling when he heard the downstairs door slam. He knew it must be Fiona. No one managed to slam doors quite so distinctively as she. He had scarcely moved since the two police officers had left and he didn't move now as he heard her running up the stairs. Suddenly the door was flung open and there she was staring down at him with an anxious expression.

'Something's happened, love. I can feel it. I've known it all the evening. I can see it in your face.'

'The police have been here,' he said dully. 'Someone saw me leave Harry Green's house.'

'Who? Who can possibly have seen you?'

'I've no idea. Anyway, I don't mean it was someone who knew me.'

'Then you've got nothing to worry about.'

'They also found the money. They've taken it away.'

'They've no right to,' she said indignantly. 'You must demand it back. The police'll try anything. They mustn't be allowed to get away with it.'

'They took it without even bothering to count it.'

'Most pigs are corrupt,' she said scornfully.

'They gave me a receipt.'

'It doesn't prove anything. They'll probably say you forged it.'

Brian bit nervously at his lower lip while Fiona gazed down at him with the expression of an anxious mother at the bedside of a sick child. After a short while, he moved his head to meet her look.

'Do you think I should run away?'

For a second, Fiona looked at him aghast.

'Oh no, love, you mustn't run away,' she said vehemently. 'Anyway, where would you run to?'

'Anywhere. It's not difficult to hide oneself. People are always doing it.'

'And always getting caught as well. It's probably just the thing the pigs want you to do.' She became thoughtful for a moment. 'If it becomes necessary for you to hide, we'll arrange it. I'll speak to Roscoe. He'll know what's best.'

Brian said nothing. In his own mind, he knew he'd run away long before he entrusted his fate to any of her lot.

But perhaps she was right. The moment to vanish hadn't come. Not yet, anyway.

CHAPTER THIRTEEN

The next day had a tentative air about it. Brian had dreaded going back to the Blackstone, but, having decided to continue normally for the time being, he had given himself no choice.

Once he was there and going about his usual duties, he

felt better, for there is nothing more reassuring to a nervous spirit than routine. And as it was Talbot's day off, he had more than enough to keep him busy. He had several occasions to see the secretary and never once did Colonel Tatham give any indication of being aware of recent police interest in the club's assistant wine steward.

But with the end of the day, his fears returned so that he found excuses to stay on awhile in the snug cocoon which the Blackstone's ambience provided. When he did come to leave, the urge not to return home was even stronger and he decided to wander around the West End for a time.

Closing the staff door behind him, he walked across a small yard which was largely taken up with dustbins and let himself out of the wicket gate into the alley which ran down one side of the club premises. He noticed a car parked directly opposite the end, but there was nothing unusual about that. As he walked towards it, the passenger door nearest to him opened and Detective Sergeant Hanson got out.

Brian had only five yards to go and wondered whether to make a dash for it, but, even in the same split second, realised it would be a futile action. As it was, he and Hanson came face to face at the alley's entrance. Hanson spoke and for a moment Brian didn't think he could be hearing aright. The police officer's voice was quiet and conversational, but what he said made Brian feel as though all his bones had suddenly liquified.

'I'm arresting you on suspicion of having murdered one Harry Green...'

There was more, but Brian was in no condition to take it in. Hanson opened the rear door of the car and ushered him in.

'O.K. Tom,' Sergeant Hanson said to the driver, 'back to the station.'

For several minutes, Brian stared out bemused, unable

to assemble his thoughts or speak. Then he became aware that Sergeant Hanson was saying something about an identification parade.

Brian shook his head as though to clear it. 'Can you say that again?'

'When we get to the station, you'll be asked to go on an identification parade,' Hanson said, watching him covertly.

'Oh! And if I refuse?'

'That'll be up to Detective Chief Superintendent Chivers. He's the officer in charge of the case.'

'Because you can't make me go on a parade.'

'Quite right! Though it's always seemed to me the lesser of two evils from the suspect's point of view. You do have a sporting chance on a parade, but if you refuse a direct confrontation can be arranged. Anyway, the choice is yours.'

'I shall refuse everything until I've seen a lawyer.'

Sergeant Hanson laughed. 'That's got a familiar ring about it. They all say that. Well, almost all! Certainly all who've had a bit of trouble before.' He gave Brian an amused look. 'Perhaps your luck'll hold again. Twice you've managed to wriggle through the sieve, I'm told.'

'I've been found not guilty by a jury twice.'

'Same thing, except I call it wriggling through the sieve. This time you may find the holes a bit smaller.'

Brian turned his head to look out of the window. It was his experience that the more confident the police seemed, the warier you needed to become. And Sergeant Hanson was exuding confidence. Curiously, he found his own spirits rising. The suspense of wondering what was going to happen was over. Proof again that anticipation is the worst part of any ordeal.

'Suspicion of having murdered...' Wasn't that what Sergeant Hanson had said? Not, I'm arresting you on a charge of murdering ... But, on suspicion of having murdered. At the back of Brian's mind, there was something he'd been told by a fellow prisoner when he'd last been on remand at Brixton prison. It was that the police couldn't hold you on suspicion, they either had to charge you or let you go. He decided to probe this delicate question.

'Did you say you were arresting me on suspicion?' he asked, with a frown.

'That's exactly what I said.'

'I don't think you're allowed to.'

Sergeant Hanson stared at him in surprise. 'Then think again, because I am. Are you trying to teach me my own job!'

'Somebody either has to be charged or let go,' Brian said, doggedly.

'Near enough right. And that's what'll happen.'

'You mean I may not be charged?'

'Correct.'

'And if I'm not, I shall be released.'

'Correct. If.'

'What's it depend on?'

'Mostly on whether you're picked out on the identification parade. But not entirely.'

'Go on!'

'Go on, indeed! Cheeky monkey!'

The car turned in under an archway and pulled up in the familiar surroundings of a police station yard. Sergeant Hanson jumped out and held the door open for Brian. Then steering him lightly by the elbow, they passed through the rear entrance to the station, went along a corridor, up a flight of stairs and along another corridor until they reached a door labelled 'Detective Chief Superintendent'. Hanson knocked and they both entered.

'Here's Tanner, sir,' he said, as though claiming the prize in a treasure hunt.

Detective Chief Superintendent Chivers studied Brian impassively.

'Sit down, Tanner. Or do I call you Brian or perhaps even Mr Tanner?'

Brian shrugged.

'Let's stick to Tanner then. You know why you've been brought here?'

'He doubts the legality of his arrest, sir,' Hanson broke in.

'How's that?'

'Doesn't believe there's any power to arrest on suspicion.'

'Well, there is, Tanner. The law gives me a reasonable time to decide whether to charge you or release you. At this moment, however, you're under arrest on suspicion of having murdered Harry Green. One of the things that'll help confirm or remove the suspicion is an identification parade. Are you willing to take part in one?'

'Doesn't seem I have much choice.'

'I take that as assent. In which event we'll get one fixed up right away. It'll take a bit of time, so while we're waiting I want to ask you some questions. But first let me remind you that you're still under caution. You understand that?'

'I don't remember Sergeant Hanson cautioning me, but I suppose he'll say he did.'

Hanson flushed. 'I cautioned him in the car, sir, before we ever drew away from the kerb. D.C. Kent can corroborate.'

'To remove all doubt in Tanner's mind, just caution him again would you?'

Sergeant Hanson intoned the familiar words in a wooden tone as though reciting something learnt as an imposition.

'Right,' Detective Chief Superintendent Chivers said briskly, 'question one. Did you know Harry Green?'

'I don't know anyone of that name.'

'Have you ever been to number forty-two Hersholt Street?'

'No.'

'Sure?'

'I'm sure.'

'Where were you between eight and ten o'clock last Tuesday night?'

Brian put on a thoughtful expression.

'I came off duty at eight o'clock and I wandered around the West End for about an hour before going home.'

'Go anywhere particular?'

'I had a pint of beer at the Duke's Head.'

'Where's that?'

'I don't know the name of the street. It's just off Leicester Square.'

'Meet anyone you knew?'

'No.'

'Often go to that particular pub?'

'Fairly.'

'Crowded, was it?'

'Yes.'

Chivers leaned back in his chair and gave Brian a long appraising look. Brian returned the look. So far he had not slipped up and both of them knew it. He had said nothing which could be disproved, other than by some freakish chance.

'I think,' Chivers said, in a thoughtful sort of tone, 'that we'll defer further questioning until after the identification parade. Like a cup of tea while we're waiting?'

Soon after Brian had finished his tea, the phone on Chivers' desk rang. Chivers lifted the receiver, listened for a second, said 'Thank you' and replaced it.

'Everything's ready,' he said, getting up. 'Been on an identification parade before, Tanner?' Brian shook his head. 'Inspector Holmes of the uniform branch will be in charge. He'll explain everything to you. I'll see you again afterwards.'

Sergeant Hanson led the way downstairs and handed

Brian over to Inspector Holmes, a tall, lean-looking officer who reminded him of a schoolmaster.

'Sit down a moment, Tanner,' the inspector said, 'while I explain things to you. The parade consists of eleven men and you'll make the twelfth. They're near enough all your age and most of them also have long hair like you.' He gave Brian a wintry smile which accentuated his schoolmasterish appearance. 'You can pick your own position and you can change it before each new witness is introduced to the parade.'

'You mean there's more than one?' Brian exclaimed.

'Two.'

'Who's the second?'

'Look, Tanner, I'm merely in charge of the parade. Which witnesses attend is none of my business. Now to continue. Each witness will be told to walk the full length of the parade and then to go and touch with his hand the person he thinks he recognises. If he doesn't recognise anyone, he'll say so. He'll then be led off the parade and he'll be given no opportunity of communicating with the next witness who will be waiting to go through the same procedure. Is that all clear?'

'Yes.'

'Then let's go.' As he led the way out of the room, he turned and said, 'We're holding it in the canteen, so we don't want to prolong matters unnecessarily, as it prevents officers enjoying the normal facilities.'

Brian bit off the sour comment which came to his lips. You never knew when what you said wouldn't turn up in evidence and be twisted against you.

The eleven men who had been awaiting Brian's arrival gazed at him with avid interest as he entered the room. He looked at each one of them in turn and then chose a position next to a young man who bore the greatest super-ficial resemblance to himself.

'Good luck, mate,' his neighbour said companionably as he took his place in the line.

'No talking, please,' Inspector Holmes called out primly. 'Now if we're all ready, I'll have the first witness introduced to the parade.'

'Like a bloody school photograph,' Brian's neighbour observed. 'Wonder he didn't say, all look this way and smile.'

At a sign from Inspector Holmes, the door at the further end of the canteen was opened and George Pratt came through with the sprightliness of a boxer coming out of his corner for round one. Most of those on the parade turned to look at him and Brian decided to do so, too.

This must be the man who saw me leave the house, he thought. But he can't have got much of a view of me. It was dark. Surely he won't be able to recognise me again! I've certainly never seen *him* in my life before.

Pratt made his way along the line, examining each face intently as he passed. There was something relentlessly eager about his expression which Brian found frightening.

He reached the end and came back to where Brian was standing.

'Him,' he said with a note of triumph stabbing Brian's chest with his forefinger.

'Thank you, Mr Pratt,' Inspector Holmes said smoothly. 'No, not that one, would you mind leaving by that other door.'

With George Pratt's departure, a ripple of nervous conversation broke out.

'Bad luck, mate,' Brian's neighbour said in a sympathetic voice. 'You better try somewhere different next time. I brought you bad luck.'

'No talking, please,' Inspector Holmes called out again.

'Bloody nerve! Who's doing who the favour, I'd like to know! Go on, you better move.'

'No, I'll stay here,' Brian announced. If fate was going

to play him shabby tricks, it'd play them wherever he was standing.

Once more they all turned their gaze towards the door through which the next witness was about to appear. Brian assumed it would be someone else he had never seen before. Someone else who had glimpsed his hurried departure from 42 Hersholt Street.

But when the door opened there came through it the surly-looking proprietor of the café where Brian and Harry Green had held their two meetings.

He walked along the line with a glowering expression and then unhesitatingly returned to where Brian was standing and gave him a smart tap on the shoulder.

'This man,' he declared, staring straight into Brian's face.

Brian felt he'd been kneed in the crotch. He had an urge to be sick on the floor.

'Don't give up hope, mate,' his neighbour said, 'but, all the same, you better get yourself a good lawyer.'

A few minutes later, still dazed by what had happened, Brian found himself back in Detective Chief Superintendent Chivers' room. Sergeant Hanson was also present, together with another officer whom Brian had not seen before, but whose appearance was anything but reassuring.

'This is Detective Inspector Gilroy,' Chivers said, rubbing his hands together in a satisfied way. 'Now, Brian, I think it's time you and I had a further talk...'

Previously it was Tanner; now, it's Brian. That's ominous for a start, Brian reflected. They're going to charge me with Harry Green's murder, that's for sure. They're going to charge me even though I'm innocent. The bloody injustice of it! And how can I be certain I'll get off. After all, if the bloody system acquits you twice of things you did do, the odds are it'll convict you of something you haven't done.

As this bitter line of thinking passed through his mind, he became aware that Detective Chief Superintendent Chivers was watching him with an expression of quiet interest.

'I'd give more than a penny for your thoughts at this moment,' he said. 'They look interesting.'

Brian said nothing and, after a brief silence, Chivers went on, 'Are you still saying, Brian, that you've never heard of Harry Green?'

'Yes.'

'Even after one witness has picked you out as the person who was seen running away from the house just after the murder and another has identified you as the person who was with Harry Green in his café on two occasions?'

'The first man's mistaken. I was never at that house.'

'And the second?'

'I think I recognised him, too. I've been to his café.'

'When?'

'I can't remember when.'

'A week ago? A month ago? Several months ago?'

'About a month ago perhaps.'

'Who did you go there with?'

'A bloke I know.'

'Name?'

'Stan.'

'Stan who?'

'I only know him as Stan.'

'Where does he live?'

'I don't know.'

'Where did you first meet him?'

'In a pub.'

'And how did you come to meet him in this café?'

'I happened to run into him in the street after I'd left work and we went in there for a cup of tea and a chat.'

'And what was the reason for meeting him there again later?'

'He suggested it.'

'Why?'

'I can't tell you.'

'You're making it all up, aren't you, Brian?' Chivers said slowly.

'No.'

In the silence which followed, Brian decided that he had adopted a good line in admitting knowledge of the café proprietor, but denying any connection with the house in which the murder had taken place. Something in Chivers' manner, moreover, seemed to confirm this. He glanced at the other two officers in the room. Inspector Gilroy was glowering as though impatient at the way the interview was going. Sergeant Hanson was sitting forward on his chair with a watchful expression.

Chivers spoke again. 'From the scene of the murder, it looked as though there'd been a struggle. It could be that Green was the aggressor, in which event what looks like a case of murder could turn out to be manslaughter at the most.'

Sly bastard, Brian thought. Trying to get me to admit it on that basis.

'Have you followed me?' Chivers asked.

'Yes.'

'And?'

'I don't know whether it was murder or manslaughter or anything else you like to call it, because I wasn't there when it happened.'

Chivers sighed. 'You could be making things more difficult for yourself than they need be.'

'I'm telling the truth.'

Inspector Gilroy made a derisive noise. 'Here's Mr Chivers doing his best to help you and all you do is feed us a string of lies.' His tone clearly indicated that, if he were in charge of the interview, it would be conducted with a good deal less indulgence towards the suspect.

Chivers leaned forward and said, 'Perhaps you can explain, Brian, how Harry Green's fingerprints got on some of the bank notes found at your place?'

Brian blinked. It was the last thing he'd expected at that moment. Now he knew why they hadn't counted the money! They hadn't wanted to impart their own prints or spoil any that might already be there. But body-blow of a question as it undoubtedly was, his mind was now in top gear and he was thinking more quickly all the time.

'It depends on whether Harry Green is the person I know as Stan,' he said.

'And if he is?'

'Stan handed me some money at our last meeting.'

'How much?'

'Twenty-five pounds.'

'For what purpose?'

'It was a repayment.'

'A repayment for what?'

'I'd rather not say.'

'Even your fertile brain beginning to dry up, is it?' Chivers asked with a tigerish smile.

'It's not that at all.'

'Come on, Brian, if there is an answer, you'd better produce it. But if, as I suspect, you've run out of answers, I'll just draw my own conclusions.'

'If you're not going to believe me, anyway, there's no point in my telling you.'

Chivers looked annoyed. 'Don't try that fancy talk on me! I've been very patient so far, but there are limits.'

'Look, Tanner, we know you did it,' Gilroy broke in, 'so why don't you give us the truth? If you help us, we'll help you. But go on playing silly buggers and you'll wish your mother had never conceived you.'

'Why don't you do yourself a good turn, Brian,' Sergeant

Hanson said from the other side of the room, 'and tell the truth from the beginning?'

'All I'd like at this moment is an answer to that last question,' Chivers said in an obvious bid to re-assert his authority.

'All right,' Brian said, 'I'll answer the question. I'd lent him twenty-five pounds and he was repaying me.'

'You'd lent him twenty-five pounds?' Chivers asked in plain disbelief.

'Yes.'

'Why couldn't you have said so at once?' Brian shrugged. 'Well, why not? Unless you were trying to think of a better story!'

This was so close to the truth that Brian decided it best to assume a stolid expression and wait for the next question.

'Well, let's probe this a little further,' Chivers said in a hostile voice. 'When had you lent him this money?'

'When we met on the first occasion.'

'Why did he want it?'

'He didn't say. Just that it was very urgent and he'd return it in a few days.'

'Let me get this clear. You happen to run into this chap you know as Stan in the street. You accompany him to a café and you lend him twenty-five quid.'

'That's right.'

'Do you frequently lend large sums of money—well, they're large to a mere police officer, but perhaps not to you—to virtual strangers?'

'No.'

'Ever done so before?'

'No-o.'

'Then why on this occasion?'

'Because he asked for it and I trusted him and because I happened to have it on me.'

'Curious that you were carrying the very sum he wanted!'

'He wanted more, but that was all I had,' Brian replied, trying to keep a note of triumph from his voice. He'd come back quickly with that one.

'Wish I had a few friends like him!' Gilroy said with heavy sarcasm.

Chivers ignored the interruption. 'And after he repays you, you take the money home and put it with the rest of your so-called savings?'

'Yes.'

'I suppose these five notes would have been the ones on top of the bag?'

Fresh warning bells began to sound in Brian's mind. 'I don't recall,' he said warily.

'Well, you'd hardly have slipped them into different places in the bag, would you?' Chivers said, seizing his opening.

'I just don't remember.'

'Well, it wouldn't make sense, would it? You weren't shuffling them like cards, you were putting five five pound notes into a bag containing a lot of others. Obviously, they'd be together. It stands to reason, doesn't it?'

'I think I took the money out of the bag the next day and so they may have got mixed about then.'

'That's what you think?'

'It's possible. I just don't know.'

'I must say, Brian, I give you full marks for improvisation.'

'I don't follow.'

'For making things up as you go along,' Chivers said amiably.

'I'm telling the truth.'

'We'll see. We'll see.' The phone on his desk rang and he picked up the receiver. 'Chief Superintendent Chivers speaking ... Oh, hello, Jim ... yes, he's still here ... no,

not yet ... right, I won't do anything until you come ...
No, that's fine, there's no compelling haste ... see you in
about half an hour, then.'

After he'd rung off, he turned to Detective Sergeant
Hanson. 'Take Brian downstairs and give him a meal. I
expect he could do with a break.'

Brian got up and paused tentatively in front of Chivers'
desk. 'I want a solicitor,' he said.

'I wondered when he'd pull that one,' Gilroy observed.

'There'll be time enough for that later,' Chivers said.

'I want one now. I know my rights.'

'And I know mine, too! Off you go and have your meal.'

'How much longer are you going to keep me here?'

'You'll find out.'

With that, Chivers rose and walked out of the room,
leaving Brian no choice, but to follow Sergeant Hanson
who was waiting by the door. He was taken to a cell on
the ground floor and locked in by a uniformed sergeant.
A few minutes later another officer brought him a plate
of steaming food.

'You won't find better grub in London,' the officer said,
cheerfully.

After he had gone, Brian stared at the plate without
enthusiasm. Then he speared a cube of meat and began
thoughtfully chewing it. He was still certain he was going
to be charged and he didn't understand why it hadn't
already taken place. Perhaps, after all, they were short of a
few pieces of evidence. The fact that they were making a
ghastly mistake in thinking he'd murdered Harry Green
was no solace. Such mistakes did happen. Why, innocent
men had even been hanged, or so it was later said! At
least, he could no longer suffer that grim fate. He thought
back over the recent interrogation. On the whole, he
thought he had coped with it reasonably well. It didn't
matter that they knew he had lied as long as they couldn't
prove it. The alternative had been to refuse to say any-

thing at all. If he'd said nothing, they'd have assumed his guilt immediately and it would all have looked much worse later on in court. It was no good the lawyers saying smugly that the prosecution had to prove its case and that the defendant had every right to maintain his silence. The fact was that if you didn't answer what were regarded as reasonable questions you were sunk, with your precious right of silence still nailed to the masthead. The whole system was one gigantic lottery with too many people trying to fiddle the result.

A key turned in the lock and the officer who had brought him his meal appeared in the doorway.

'You haven't finished it,' he said, with a note of genuine concern.

'I wasn't hungry.'

'You can't have been. Normally, people hammer on the door for second helpings. Anyway, here's Sergeant Hanson to take you back upstairs.'

Detective Chief Superintendent Chivers was sitting at his desk as they entered, but, on the chair previously occupied by Detective Inspector Gilroy, there now sat Detective Chief Superintendent Samson.

' 'Evening, Brian,' Samson said. 'If you're wondering what I'm doing here, the answer is I'm still looking for snuff-boxes, or, perhaps I should say, the person or persons who spirited them out of the Blackstone Club. I think you may be able to help.'

'I've told you all I know.'

Ignoring the fact that he'd spoken, Samson went on, 'This man Green who's been murdered was your accomplice, wasn't he? It was he who contacted you about stealing the snuff-boxes. That's right, isn't it?'

'No.' Brian's throat felt tight and the monosyllable came with difficulty.

'You see, we now know quite a bit about Harry Green. It was just the sort of job he might try and pull if someone put him up to it. I believe someone did put him up to it and that he enlisted your help.'

'It's not true.'

'But you did know him previously?'

Brian's spirit groaned. That was one lie which had lost no time in coming home to roost.

'You've told Mr Chivers you first met him in a pub some time ago. I'm suggesting that he got into contact with you again shortly before the burglary. That's right, isn't it?'

'No.'

'Was Talbot in on it as well?'

'No.'

'You mean that you were, but he wasn't?'

'No, no!'

'Come on, Brian, it's time you told the truth. Tell me the truth now and I'll do all I can to help you.'

Brian had the sensation of being swept out to sea by the tide of questions, but he knew he must not allow himself to go under. Suddenly, as he was casting his mind frantically over the last few minutes, his heart gave a small joyful leap. Samson couldn't have a single fact to go on. All his questions must have been based on guesswork. It was uncomfortably accurate guesswork for the most part, but if he'd had evidence at his disposal, it would surely have become apparent. That must be right and, if so, it meant Samson would depart as empty-handed as he came.

'I've told you all I can,' he said with a helpless shrug.

'That money found in your room, it was your pay-off, wasn't it? How much were you paid for your part in the affair?'

'No.'

'A jury'll never believe it was your savings, particularly when they hear of Harry Green's fingerprints being found on part of the money.'

'I've already explained that.'

'Yes, but now let's hear the truth for a change.'

Brian's head throbbed with the word. It seemed every-one in the room was mouthing 'truth' at him. Surely they'd have to give up soon. Once it was clear to them that they were going to get nothing further from him.

Suddenly, Samson rose from his chair.

'I'll be seeing you again,' he said, with a note of grim-ness as he walked to the door.

Chivers accompanied him out into the passage, clos-ing the door behind them.

'Glad I'm not in your shoes,' Sergeant Hanson remarked when they were alone.

'Why?'

'I should have thought that was obvious. You'll be want-ing our help and you won't get it. We only help people who co-operate with us.'

'You mean, who make confessions, even if they haven't done it.'

Hanson shook his head. 'Nobody makes false confessions unless they're barmy. And you're not barmy. Just obsti-nate. Foolish and obstinate, that's what you are.'

Brian met his gaze and they stared at each other like two strange cats. Brian was thankful he'd had previous experience of police interrogation and that he knew the various tricks they employed. The swift changes of tack from quiet bullying to cajoling and appeals to conscience.

O.K., so they had their job to do! But that was no reason why he had to make it any easier for them where he was the centre of the interest.

Detective Chief Superintendent Chivers came back into the room and Brian steeled himself for another bout of questioning. But Chivers didn't sit down. He went across to a filing cabinet and pulled out one of the drawers. Then, over his shoulder as though he was suddenly aware they were still there, he said:

'Take him downstairs, Sergeant, and have him charged with the murder of Harry Green. Then come back to my room.'

'With the prisoner, sir?'

'Without him.'

Five minutes later when Hanson returned and reported completion of his instructions, Chivers said, 'We are now going to set about disproving, one by one, each—and I mean each—of the dozen or more lies he has told us. I'd like a typed copy of the note you took of the interview as soon as possible and I shall then identify and number each and every lie he's felt bold enough to throw in our faces.'

'Yes, sir,' Hanson said with a quick nod. He'd seldom seen his Detective Chief Superintendent in such a mood of savage determination.

'If necessary,' Chivers went on, 'I'll supply the jury with a chart showing his lies, each one picked out in a different colour.'

Hanson gave a nervous laugh. 'We've got a fairly good case against him anyway, sir.'

'It's going to be a lot better by the time I've finished with it.'

CHAPTER FOURTEEN

When Fiona arrived home to find no Brian, she was not unduly concerned and assumed he was out drinking somewhere. When she awoke in the middle of the night and he was still not there, she wondered whether he had, after all, taken it into his head to run away. But she was sure morning would reveal what had happened and that there would be some comfortable explanation. That is, if explanation were called for, because he might well be back by then.

But when morning did come and there was still no sign of him, nor yet any phone call, her feeling of anxiety increased rapidly.

At ten o'clock she went down to the coin-box telephone in the hall of the house and made a call to the Blackstone.

Though she had never met him, she knew the odds were that, at that hour, it would be answered by Talbot.

'Is that the Blackstone Club?' she asked when she heard a male voice at the other end of the line.

'Yes, Blackstone Club here.'

'Is that Mr Talbot?'

'Yes. Who is that speaking?'

'I'm a friend of Brian Tanner's. I'm worried about him and I wondered if you knew where he was. He didn't come home last night.'

'Are you the young lady he lives with?'

'Yes.'

'Well, he didn't come home because he's been arrested and charged with murder.' Talbot's tone was spiteful. 'A nice bit of trouble he's caused us. And all on a day when we have two lunch parties. I don't know how we're going to manage. If I may say so, miss, he seems to have let *everyone* down.'

A moment later there was a click as Talbot cut her off. Fiona let out a stifled cry and rushed back upstairs where she threw herself down on the bed and allowed her grief to pour out in noisy, uncontrollable sobs. Eventually, sheer exhaustion rendered her still and silent.

She rose, not daring to look at herself in the mirror, and put on her afghan coat and hurried from the room. Twenty minutes later she arrived at the house where Hive, Roscoe and Arthur camped out in disregarded squalor.

Only Hive was there when she burst into their room.

'The fascist pigs have arrested Brian,' she said, panting.

116

A look of annoyance mixed with anxiety crossed Hive's face. 'Well, go on,' he said sharply.

'He's been charged with murder.'

'Who on earth is he supposed to have murdered?'

'Some man he hardly knows, but he didn't do it. It's a frame-up by the fascist pigs.'

'Look, Fiona, hadn't you better tell me everything? All our positions could be jeopardised if Tanner talks.'

Fiona stared at him in amazement. 'It's my Brian we're speaking of. He won't give anything away.'

'I certainly hope not, but I don't necessarily share your confidence. So now tell me everything and then I'll decide what's best.'

'We've got to set him free,' she said fiercely. 'I can't live without him.'

Hive frowned. 'Pull yourself together, Fiona. Important things are at stake and it's no time for hysterics.'

'You don't understand how I miss him. He means every-thing to me.'

'It just shows how bourgeois you've become,' he said darkly. 'You're merely giving your emotions a field day. All you're going to miss is his cock and you know it. It's the sort of schoolgirl infatuation you should have grown out of years ago. You really make me very impatient when you carry on like this.'

For answer, Fiona sank on to the mattress, which was Roscoe's bed, and buried her head in her hands while Hive observed her with scorn.

It was at this moment that Roscoe returned to the room. He paused just inside the door and glanced from Fiona's slumped form to Hive.

'Her Brian has been picked up for murder,' Hive said caustically, 'which doesn't say a lot for her choice of boy-friends.'

'Brian murdered someone?' Roscoe said with a small smile of disbelief. 'Who in God's name?'

'She's in such a state, she can't get two words out without indulging in an orgy of emotion. I'm still waiting to hear.'

Roscoe walked across to Fiona and squatted down beside her.

'Come on, girl, we've got to know all you can tell us. Anyway, that's why you came, wasn't it, to tell us? You'll feel better when you have.'

She took her hands away from her face and in stammered sentences told them the whole story of Brian's involvement with Harry Green and the theft of the snuff-boxes.

'Oh, my God!' Roscoe said when she had finished, shaking his head reproachfully. 'He really has shit himself.'

'It's what he may do to the rest of us that gripes me,' Hive broke in. 'We'll have to get a message to him somehow, telling him to clam up so far as we're concerned. If it isn't too late!'

'You needn't worry,' Fiona said, indignantly. 'Brian won't tell them a thing about us. Anyway, when I visit him, I'll ...'

'That's out of the question,' Hive said sharply.

'What do you mean?'

'I'm afraid you can't visit him. Surely you can see that! Once you start appearing at court when he's up or skimming off down to Brixton prison, we might as well all go and parade up and down with banners.' He shook his head angrily. 'I must say, he couldn't have chosen a worse time to ball things up.'

Fiona shot to her feet, eyes blazing. 'All you do is think of yourselves! Nobody thinks of him, framed by the pigs for a crime he hasn't committed. All the Blackstone is worried about is their stupid lunch parties. And you're as bad. I came here expecting sympathy and help and all I get are petulant reproaches. I hate you all.'

She made to rush out of the room, but Roscoe barred

her way and put an arm round her shoulder.

'Keep your cool, girl. I'll make you a cup of coffee.'

Hive, meanwhile, began pacing up and down the room, his brow furrowed in a heavy frown. In Fiona's experience, it was the expression which usually preceded one of his declamatory outbursts. All she knew this time was that if he began declaiming against Brian, she'd walk out and never see any of them again ever. Ever!

Thanks to Talbot, news of Brian's arrest spread rapidly through the Blackstone. By lunchtime, there wasn't a person on the premises who hadn't heard what had happened.

One of the first members to be given the news was ex-Judge Whitby-Stansford. He had, as usual, arrived as the club opened and had scarcely ensconced himself in the smoking-room to begin his leisurely perusal of *The Times* when Talbot entered.

'What a terrible thing about Brian, isn't it, sir?' Talbot remarked, peering over the top of the paper at the ex-judge behind it.

'Who's Brian?' ex-Judge Whitby-Stansford asked, in a tone which would have discouraged anyone but Talbot on this particular day.

'My young assistant in the wine pantry. Brian Tanner.'

'Oh!'

'I don't expect you've heard then, sir?'

'Heard what?'

'The police have arrested him.'

Ex-Judge Whitby-Stansford put down his newspaper and glanced up sharply. 'You mean for the theft of the snuff-boxes?'

Talbot shook his head. 'No, he's killed someone. It's murder.'

'Nothing to do with the snuff-boxes?'

'I wouldn't be surprised if that follows, sir.'

'What makes you say that?'

'I always felt there was something funny about that young man. I never really trusted him. I was telling Colonel Tatham so this morning.'

'Seemed quite an obliging youth to me, but I expect you saw more of him than I did.'

'Anyway, it's not very nice for the club.'

'Who's he supposed to have murdered?'

'A man called Green.'

'Oh, well, I expect you'll find a replacement soon.'

'Not soon enough. We've got two private lunch parties today. I hardly know which way to turn.'

Ex-Judge Whitby-Stansford let out a grunt which might have been one of sympathy or dismissal.

Talbot interpreted it as both and set off to find another early arrival to whom he could impart the news. To his annoyance, however, he found the hall porter button-holing members as they entered. He was holding audience by the front-door and ignored Talbot's glance of disapproval.

Sir John Pearn arrived at lunchtime and went straight to the secretary's room.

'Anything further to what you told me on the phone?' he said, pulling up a chair and sitting down.

'No, Sir John. I gather he came up at court this morning and was remanded in custody for a week.'

'That's standard. I don't doubt that he was also granted legal aid.'

'Do you think we ought to get in touch with him?'

'Who's we?'

'The Club in the person of myself.'

'With what object?'

'Seeing if there's anything we ought to do for him.'

'Such as?'

Colonel Tatham, who had had little to do with lawyers before being appointed secretary to the Blackstone Club, found it peculiarly irksome to be on the receiving end of this type of cross-examination. There were a number of members, apart from the Chairman, who were wont to slip into what he assumed to be their court-room manner. A few of them never seemed to slip out of it.

'In the army, it's an officer's responsibility to look after his men, particularly when they're in trouble,' he said frostily.

'The comparison is irrelevant,' Sir John replied. 'But there's no harm in someone paying him a welfare visit if that's what you have in mind. Perhaps Talbot would go.'

'I don't think so.'

'Oh?'

'Talbot didn't care for him. Or so he now tells me.'

'A pity we didn't trust Talbot's instinct earlier.'

'I think it's what lawyers would call post facto instinct, Sir John.'

Sir John Pearn gave a sniff. 'Did you get in touch with Samson after phoning me?'

'Yes. I gather he'd interrogated Tanner, but without success.'

'Did he think this man's murder and our theft were in any way connected?'

'He wasn't inclined to speculate.'

'Of course, if they are, we need to show considerable circumspection in any contact we have with Tanner. So far as the murder goes, the Club's stance is, in one sense, neutral. But that certainly isn't so where our own property is concerned.'

'Quite so.'

'And naturally I'm a good deal more interested in the recovery of our snuff-boxes and the punishment of those involved in the theft, than I am in the death of someone who is nothing more to me than a name. Green, did you say it was?'

'Yes. Harry Green.'

'I trust the police are finding out whether there's any link between Green and our stolen property.'

'I imagine they are.'

'I'll have a word with Samson myself when I get out of court this afternoon.' Sir John became thoughtful for a second. 'Actually, I've got another officer coming to see me at half past four to discuss security arrangements for the trial of this man Gregor Maltby at the Old Bailey next week. If Samson is free, he might come along about the same time. Give him a ring, will you, and then leave a message for me at the R.C.J.'

'R.C.J.?'

'Good lord, Tatham, haven't you learnt that bit of legal nomenclature yet? Royal Courts of Justice. If he can't come along, tell him to phone me in my room there. It's extension 3427.' He stood up. 'What about a drink before lunch?'

The two men made their way downstairs to the bar where their arrival was greeted by a display of nonchalant curiosity.

That evening the Feelys were entertaining another couple to dinner at the club. Arnold Feely was in the bar when his wife arrived and he went to join her in the 'common-room', one of the few rooms in which women were permitted to set foot.

'Aren't they going to put something in the cases where the snuff-boxes used to be?' Marcia Feely said, after he had fetched her a gin and tonic.

'In due course.'

'It looks terrible at the moment with all that empty space.'

'The committee's waiting to see if any of them are recovered before deciding what to put in their place.'

'How very optimistic!' She opened her bag, pulled out a small platinum case and selected a cigarette. Her husband leaned forward with his lighter and their eyes met and held for a second.

'What sort of day have you had?' Feely asked, settling back into his chair.

'Busy. Most of it spent in arranging to ship some things over to the States. The number of bits of paper you have to fill in positively encourages dishonesty.'

'Seen Sid Craddock recently?'

'As a matter of fact he looked in this afternoon,' she said, studying the tip of her cigarette as though it were an object of rare interest.

'What did he have to say?'

'He just said everything was fine with him and he hoped it was with us, too.'

'Was this at the shop?'

'Of course. Where else?'

'I thought it might have been at the flat.'

Marcia gave her husband a strange look which revealed nothing of what was passing through her mind. Then her face broke into a sudden welcoming smile and she said, 'Here are Isabel and Joe.'

Feely jumped up to get chairs for their guests and then went in search of drinks.

'Such excitements at Arnold's club!' Isabel said eagerly. 'It's in the paper almost every day.

'Over the theft of the snuff-boxes you mean?' Marcia said.

'Yes, and now this young man being charged with murder.'

Marcia Feely put on an expression of polite interest. 'Arnold hasn't told me about that.'

Feely reappeared and Isabel said, 'Marcia doesn't know anything about your further drama.'

'What further drama are you talking about?'

'The club servant who's been charged with murder.'

'No, you never told me,' Marcia chimed in.

'He'd only been here a short time.'

'Will one of the members defend him?' Isabel bubbled on.

'I've no idea.'

'Wouldn't that be unethical?' Joe enquired.

'Not necessarily.'

'But supposing the judge knew him?'

'Then he'd disqualify himself from trying the case.'

'I'm always telling people that I shall have you to defend me, Arnold, when I'm in trouble,' Isabel said. 'You would defend me, wouldn't you?'

'I'm sure you'll never get into trouble.'

'But supposing I did?'

'Lawyers never answer hypothetical questions.'

There was laughter and Joe said, 'Isabel watches all those T.V. courtroom dramas and always ends up identifying herself with the accused.'

'It's my feeling for the underdog.'

'I doubt whether a psychiatrist would give you such a comforting explanation,' her husband observed, dryly.

'The theft of the Blackstone's snuff-boxes would make a wonderful T.V. thriller,' Isabel went on with undiminished enthusiasm. 'How on earth was it done?'

'I've no idea,' Arnold Feely said, with a faintly set smile.

'But you must have a theory?'

'None.'

'I don't call that very enterprising of you. What do you think, Marcia?'

'I'm afraid I haven't thought about it either.'

'It'd be a joke if the thief tried to sell you the snuff-boxes not knowing your connection with the club.'

Marcia Feely's tone was sharp when she spoke. 'People in my line of business are frequently circulated with details of valuable stolen property so that we can be on our guard.'

'But there must be some dishonest dealers.'

'Of course there are. Just as there are dishonest lawyers and doctors and candlestickmakers.' She looked across at her husband. 'Isn't it time we went down for dinner?'

Later, after their guests had departed and the Feelys were driving home, Marcia said, 'I may have to go over to Brussels on business next week.'

'How long'll you be away?'

'Two days. Three at the most.'

'I'd be tempted to come with you if I hadn't got a trial starting at the Old Bailey. I'm defending someone in the Maltby case.'

Marcia said nothing. She wondered why her husband bothered to make observations of that sort, when there was no one but herself to hear.

CHAPTER FIFTEEN

Familiarity with his surroundings did nothing to lend enchantment when Brian found himself again in Brixton prison. His previous sojourns there while on remand had been a single week on one occasion before being granted bail and a couple of weeks the second time.

It wasn't just that one was locked in a cell from early evening until the following morning and also for a large part of the short day, but the whole enervating business of being deposited in a state of suspended animation. Though not convicted and therefore presumed to be innocent, one was deprived of one's liberty and left waiting for a decision on one's fate.

As Brian sat in his cell the day after his first, and formal, appearance in court, he reflected gloomily that, whatever the eventual outcome of his trial, he was going to be lodged in prison for a good many weeks before it took place, for he knew that people charged with murder didn't get let out on bail.

At least he was allowed visitors; though, apart from Fiona, he couldn't think of anyone who was likely to come. By now she must obviously know what had happened to him and he felt confident that she would be along that very day.

When the magistrate had asked him if he wanted legal aid, he had nodded. Later, he had indicated that he was prepared to leave it to the court to assign him a solicitor and that he had no preferences in the matter.

He had not been impressed by the firm which had represented him on the two previous occasions and on the second had felt it was despite, rather than on account of, their efforts that he had been acquitted. They clearly took on far too much work and regarded their clients as a doctor might victims of flu during an epidemic. They did the minimum for him and were behind with everything, save claiming their fees.

It was about three o'clock that day when his cell door was unlocked and an officer told him his solicitor had called to see him. Brian jumped to his feet and followed the officer. This was, indeed, a surprise. He'd not expected to meet his lawyer yet, possibly not before his second appearance in court in a week's time. Perhaps murder cases got priority. Anyway, whatever the explanation, Brian felt gratified.

The interview rooms were some distance from the cell block in which he was lodged and he had time to wonder what sort of a person he was going to meet. It might be the solicitor himself, though more likely it'd be one of his clerks on this first visit.

As Brian was ushered into the small, cheerless room, he suddenly stopped in his tracks and stared with sagging jaw, for it was a girl who was sitting, waiting for him.

She was small and almost elflike, with large, brown eyes. She began to blush as Brian continued to stare at her.

'I'm from Snaith and Co.,' she said quickly to cover her embarrassment. 'Aren't you going to sit down?'

Brian seated himself and his face broke into a slow smile. 'Hello,' he said. 'I'm sorry I stared so, but I wasn't expecting someone like you.'

The girl opened a large notebook at a blank page and reached for a ballpoint pen. 'That's all right. I'm used to it,' she said, giving him a fleeting smile. 'Well, more or less used to it.'

'Miss Snaith did you say your name was?' Brian asked, still faintly mesmerised.

'No. Snaith and Co. is the name of the firm and we've been given the legal aid certificate to defend you. Mr Snaith will be at court when you come up on remand next week. I'm merely one of his clerks. Now...'

'What's your name, miss?'

'Rosa Epton.'

'*Miss* Epton, is it?'

'Yes. Now, let's discuss your case. First, tell me the whole story from the beginning.'

As Brian spoke, she made rapid notes, covering the pages of her notebook with small, neat writing. Substantially, he gave her the same account that he had given to the police in answer to their questions. When he finished, she glanced over what she had written. Then she put down her pen and gently massaged the fingers of her writing hand.

'Anything else you can think of?'

'No.'

'If you do later recall any further details, be sure to let me know.'

Brian nodded as though to do so would become a personal commitment.

'In due course,' she went on, 'the prosecution will serve on us copies of the witnesses' statements and you will have to go through them very carefully and add your comments in the margin so that we can give counsel proper instructions at the trial.' She gave him another fleeting smile. 'But I'm sorry, you probably don't know the procedure. Let me explain. In due course, the magistrate will be invited to commit you for trial, either on the evidence of written statements which will have been served on us in advance or on the mixed evidence of statements and live witnesses, should either the prosecution or the defence want any of the witnesses to give their evidence in person at that stage. Unless we feel there's a chance of knocking the case out at the magistrates' court, which is very rare, it's usually best to let the thing go through and reserve one's fight for the trial proper.'

'Yes, I do know about that.' She glanced at him sharply. 'You have previous convictions?' she enquired in a suspicious tone.

'I've been acquitted twice.'

'I'd better hear about both times,' she said, smoothing a page of her notebook.

As she wrote, Brian watched her. Her tongue had a funny little habit of peeping out of the corner of her mouth as she reached the end of each line and he found himself waiting for it to happen. She wore no make-up and her hair, which was straight, fell forward on either side of her face as she bent forward.

'I take it that Miss Richey will be able to support some of the details you have given me?' She looked up slowly as she spoke and her gaze was resting on his face by the time she reached the end of the sentence.

'Miss Richey? Oh, Fiona. Well, yes, but I'd sooner you didn't approach her until I've had an opportunity of speaking to her first.'

Though her expression didn't alter, Brian could tell

what she was thinking and felt uncomfortable.

'It's not that I've got to persuade her what to say,' he said, lamely. 'It's just that I haven't seen her since I was arrested and it'd be fairer to her if I had a word with her first.'

'Yes, naturally,' Rosa said in a neutral voice. 'It's not an urgent matter, anyway, as it won't arise until your trial, though, of course, the defence do now have to give notice of any alibi witnesses they're proposing to call, not that she seems to fall within that category.' She gave him one of her wispy smiles. 'But perhaps you knew that, too.'

'No. No, I didn't.'

'It's very probable, of course, that the police will seek to interview Miss Richey in the hope she can give evidence for the prosecution.'

'She won't.'

Rosa leafed back through her notes, making a correction here and there and occasionally frowning in a thoughtful manner.

'The one witness we must obviously seek to discredit is the man who says he saw you running away from the scene and who picked you out on the identification parade. At the moment we don't know his name, though we shall learn it before long.' She fixed Brian with an even stare. 'According to what you've told me, he must be wrong. And if he's wrong, it's either accidental or it's malicious. That's to say, he's either genuinely mistaken or he's wilfully false. And if he's wilfully false, it means somebody is trying to frame you for the murder. Have you any ideas who it could be?'

Brian had listened to this inexorable logic knowing that it was going to end in some question he'd prefer not to have to answer. In his own mind, he was quite certain that he had been lured to Hersholt Street in order to be framed, but at the moment, and for as long as he was denying any part in the theft of the Blackstone's snuff-boxes, he couldn't assert this. He had no doubt that those who were out to frame him for murder were those behind the theft, but this again he couldn't say. The time might come when he would be compelled to shift his ground, but for the time being he had to stick to the story of events he had given to the police and repeated to Rosa.

'No,' he said, shaking his head, 'unless it was someone who knew I'd met this man, Harry Green. That is,' he added quickly, 'if Harry Green is the man I know as Stan.'

'If we knew why Harry Green was murdered, we'd know better why you've been selected for framing,' she said thoughtfully, looking at Brian. But he made no comment. 'Well, if that's all, I'll be getting back to the office.'

'Thank you for coming so soon.'

'We always try to. It doesn't seem fair on the client otherwise. I mean he's been granted legal aid, and then as far as he's concerned nothing happens for days on end. At least Mr Snaith's clients can feel someone's interested in them from the very outset.'

She got up and Brian rose, too.

'Will you be coming again?'

'I don't expect it'll be necessary. Mr Snaith'll have a talk with you when you meet at court next week.'

'Will you be there, too?'

She shrugged. 'I don't know. Depends on our commitments that day.'

'Anyway, thank you again for coming and I certainly hope we shall meet again.'

She smiled. 'You make it sound as if we're saying goodbye at the end of a party.' A second later she was gone.

When she got back to her office, she went in to see the firm's principal, Mr Snaith, a man in his mid-thirties who managed to run a successful criminal practice with an enviable air of enjoyment, spiced with detachment. He was conscientious and capable and had steered clear of the pitfalls that are apt to beset a solicitor whose clients are, for the most part, ruthlessly self-interested. This he had achieved by his own brand of ruthlessness which was to throw over any client whom he felt was trying to manipulate him.

'I'm just back from Brixton,' Rosa said. 'I think you'll enjoy defending Tanner.'

Robin Snaith gave her a quizzical smile. 'You mean you took a fancy to him?'

'I mean I think he's got a defence,' she replied primly.

'Tell me.'

When she'd finished, Snaith grimaced. 'It doesn't sound an awfully good one to me. I've never yet had an alibi defence which I personally believed in. But I gather you think this young man is telling the truth, the whole truth and nothing but the truth?'

'The truth, but probably not the whole truth,' Rosa said after a thoughtful pause.

'I don't know whether that's particularly promising.'

'It seems odd that this man picked him out so positively on the identification parade, when at best he can only have had a fleeting glimpse of whoever it was running away.'

Snaith said nothing. He knew better than to contradict her when he was not yet in a position to form any judgment of his own. Moreover, he had considerable respect for Rosa's shrewdly attuned instinct in such matters. She had joined his firm as a typist three years ago and from that had graduated to clerk in the litigation section and now to personal assistant to her principal. It was a position she had carved out for herself by ability and nothing else. Now, as Robin Snaith ruefully admitted to himself, she was rapidly becoming the one indispensable member of his staff. And there was nothing more seductive and, at the same time, more perilous than allowing any employee to become indispensable. While they were around, everything was bliss, but they only had to go down with flu or on a package holiday to Majorca, or, worst of all, leave you for good and paralysis set in immediately.

'Which day is he remanded to next week?' he asked, breaking the silence which had fallen.

'Wednesday.'

'I'll get along to court early and have a chat with him. There's not much we can do, however, until the prosecution serves some papers on us.'

'I did tell him that.'

'I don't imagine they'll be ready to seek a committal for a month or so. You might see if you can find out what sort of a timetable they have in mind. Though I don't doubt if you phone the police they'll say it all depends on the D.P.P. and, if you phone the D.P.P., you'll only be told they've not yet had a file from the police!'

'I can try, anyway.'

'Meanwhile, have your note of the interview transcribed and let me know if you think there's any enquiry we can make in the meantime.'

Rosa got up and was about to leave the room when Robin Snaith said as an afterthought, 'We can at least ask the police to let us have a copy of his written statement under caution.'

'He didn't make one.'

Snaith raised his eyebrows in comical surprise. 'That will have made him popular!'

CHAPTER SIXTEEN

The days following Rosa Epton's visit passed more slowly than Brian would have thought possible. No one came to see him and his spirits remained at floor level throughout his waking hours. Sleep was a merciful release from the raw-edged tedium, but there was a limit to the amount of sleep a healthy twenty-three-year-old could take, particularly when the body remained untired and the mind became increasingly restless.

It was on the day after Rosa had been that he received a letter. His name was printed in capitals on the envelope and he felt sure it was from Fiona. The contents were similarly printed and read:

'My own darling Brian, my heart is aching for you and you are never out of my thoughts. Please, love, be patient and understanding. I'll come and see you as soon as I can, but it is not possible yet. I know you'll understand. Don't feel neglected as I love you every second. You must know that no prison walls can keep out my love for you. Am staying with friends. F.'

So Fiona had gone to ground. That was all 'staying with friends' could mean. Hive and Roscoe must have persuaded her to move in with them and to let him rot in prison. They were the two militant ones from under whose mental domination Fiona had never strayed far. Arthur was a milder person altogether even though he held identical views.

Curiously, the effect of the letter was not to make him feel bitter, but rather wistful. He accepted that Fiona had not deserted him completely. Her letter was evidence of that and had obviously been written with a good deal of anguish. Pretending was not her strong suit and she would not have written in those terms unless she meant what she said.

The dashing of a hope was his immediate reaction. The one person from whom he had expected a visit wouldn't be coming. And that meant even emptier days ahead.

The next afternoon while on exercise, a prisoner he had never seen before fell into step beside him.

'You, Tanner?' he enquired out of the side of his mouth.

'S'right.'

'I'm going to walk ahead now. Next time round you catch me up on me left side and 'ave your right 'and ready.'

The man quickened his pace until he was four or five yards in front of Brian and then kept at that distance.

As they approached the completion of another circuit of the exercise yard, Brian increased his own pace to draw up on his fellow prisoner. There was nothing in this to excite the interest of the two officers on duty as everyone followed their own speed so that there was constant passing and lapping of the slower walkers by the brisker paced. He had to push his way between his mysterious contact and the prisoner beside him. As he did so, his contact lurched against him and Brian felt an envelope thrust into his hand.

He immediately dropped back a few paces. At the same time, without even looking at the envelope, he slipped it into his pocket.

When he got back to the hospital wing to which he had now been moved for routine observation—all prisoners on murder charges being the subject of medical reports as to their fitness to plead and as to their responsibility for what they are alleged to have done—he made for the lavatory and there in relative seclusion took the envelope from his pocket. It just had 'Brian Tanner' typed on the front. There was no address and no stamp, which meant that it had been smuggled in and had avoided censorship. Though Brian had not had any occasion to use the letter-smuggling service, he knew that it existed—at a price. With the constant comings and goings of inmates at a remand prison, it was a difficult traffic to frustrate.

The letter inside the envelope was also typed, but unsigned. It read:

'Dear Brian, It's important, *very important*, that you don't tell the police anything about you know who and her friends. Do that for us and we'll help you.'

He read it through a second time, then tore it into small pieces and flushed it down the pan.

Taken in conjunction with Fiona's letter of the previous day, it became even clearer what had happened. She'd taken refuge with her lot, who were nervous that Brian might give the police a lead to them. Well, let them believe he might, he thought in disgust! After which, he fell to wondering in what way they proposed helping him. One thing for sure, if they did help him, it would be entirely out of self-interest.

And so passed his first week in Brixton prison, relieved only by two letters and a visit from his solicitor's attractive clerk.

On the day he was due to appear in court, he woke up buoyant with expectation as though he was going on a school treat. The fact that the end of the day would, in default of miracles, find him back in the same place for another week was still insufficient to blight the prospect.

The van which was to take him and others to various

magistrates' courts set off before the rush-hour traffic had built up. The court at which Brian was to be deposited was one of the last on its round so that he had a longer ride than most. Each cell within the van had a small window and he hardly took his eyes away from the passing scene outside, restricted though his view of it was.

On arrival at court, he was placed in a cell and brought a cup of tea by a cheerful, red-faced P.C., which caused his spirits to soar even higher.

Shortly before ten o'clock, the cell door was unlocked to admit Mr Snaith.

Brian looked up enquiringly.

'My name's Snaith,' the solicitor said. 'I've been assigned to your defence.'

Brian sprang to his feet and shook the outstretched hand. 'I'm sorry, sir, I didn't realise who it was,' he said in an embarrassed tone. His previous solicitor, when he did eventually meet him, had shown no inclination to shake hands.

'No apologies called for,' Snaith said in an agreeable tone. 'I expect you know what's going to happen today. Which is virtually nothing, I'm afraid, as far as you're concerned. The police will be asking for a further remand in custody and they'll be granted it as a matter of course, though I will try and get them to say when they'll be ready to go ahead.'

'Is there any chance at all of getting bail?'

'No, none. It's never granted in murder cases save in the most compassionate circumstances and I'm afraid you can't muster any of those.' He glanced at his watch. 'I'll have another word with you afterwards before you go back to Brixton.' He pressed the bell to bring an officer to unlock the cell door and let him out. 'By the way, here are some cigarettes,' he said, chucking a packet of ten down on the table. 'Better put them in your pocket quickly or we'll both be in trouble.'

The solicitor hadn't long departed before the door was again unlocked to reveal Detective Chief Superintendent Chivers and Detective Sergeant Hanson. Brian saw no reason to get to his feet for his further visitors.

''Morning, Brian,' Chivers said. 'Everything going all right?'

'I'm still alive if that's what you mean.'

'And still pretty cheeky, too, by the sound of it,' Hanson remarked.

'Seen your solicitor yet?' Chivers enquired.

'Yes.'

'Mr Snaith, isn't it?'

'S'right.'

There was a silence while Chivers gazed abstractedly round the cell. Brian had the impression he felt inhibited by the information that his solicitor had already been to see him.

'Well, just thought I'd look in and see if everything was all right,' he said unconvincingly, as he turned about to leave.

Brian's regard for Mr Snaith and his firm went up a further notch. It was obvious that the police had a healthy respect for his name and were wary about twisting any of the rules where his clients were concerned.

For the next hour nothing happened, save that he was given another cup of tea. Then the door was unlocked by a uniformed officer, who gestured him to get up.

'Come on, your case'll be called in a minute.'

The jailer's office was the usual throng of police officers and defendants mingled in an atmosphere of subdued bedlam.

The door which led into court swung violently open every few minutes to admit the jailer and a prisoner whose case had just been dealt with.

'John Brown, ten pounds or fourteen days. No time to pay,' the jailer would sing out. Or, 'Lily O'Connell, remanded seven days for medical report.'

It was following Lily O'Connell's return from judgment that Brian was pushed forward and propelled through the door by the jailer's helping hand.

'Remand number three, your worship, Brian Tanner.'

Detective Chief Superintendent Chivers stepped into the witness box to Brian's left.

'I ask for a further remand in custody, your worship,' he said. 'The police have still got a number of enquiries to make.'

'Any objections, Mr Snaith?' the magistrate enquired in a courteous tone.

'No, sir, but I wonder if Mr Chivers can indicate when the prosecution will be ready to proceed?'

'I can't say, your worship. It depends on the Director of Public Prosecutions.'

'May I ask when you hope to send your file to him?'

'In about two weeks' time, perhaps.'

'So we may have committal proceedings in about three or four weeks?'

'Could be, but I'm not really in a position to say for certain.'

During this exchange, the magistrate's gaze had switched, as they spoke, from one to the other, rather as if he were following a not particularly exciting tennis rally.

'Satisfied, Mr Snaith?' he broke in, hopefully.

'It's difficult to be satisfied on these occasions, sir. It's like striking a rock...'

'And no water gushes forth! Or none worth speaking of, eh, Mr Snaith?'

'Precisely, sir.'

While this had been going on, Brian had glanced around the court to see if there was anyone he recognised. There was certainly no sign of Fiona, but, sitting on a bench in front of the public gallery, he'd noticed Colonel Tatham.

The secretary had given him a flicker of a smile as their eyes met.

When Brian turned to face front again, the magistrate was staring at him and the jailer hissed to him to stand up.

'You'll be remanded in custody for a further seven days, Tanner.' He looked across at Detective Chief Superintendent Chivers. 'Perhaps you'd be good enough, Chief Superintendent, to convey to those concerned that I hope these formal remands won't drag on. Indeed'—he smiled up at the ceiling—'I don't propose to allow them to do so.'

Brian was hustled back through the swing-door.

'Remanded in custody for seven days,' the jailer called out. Then, lowering his voice, he added, 'He's in one of his funny moods.'

As he returned to court with the next defendant, Chivers and Snaith entered the office together.

'I don't understand what the rush is,' Chivers said in an aggrieved tone.

'I don't like my clients languishing in prison for longer than necessary. That's all,' Snaith replied amiably.

'Hell, he's only been there a week!'

'So far!'

'Look, Mr Snaith, you're a reasonable man and you must realise the police have a hell of a lot of work preparing a case like this. I assure you we don't sit on our hands.'

'I appreciate all your difficulties, including some you possibly haven't thought of, but I still don't have to accept, without trying to do something about it, that a client of mine should be forced to squander even a tiny fraction of his life in custody before any evidence is heard against him.'

'I gave evidence of arrest at the first hearing,' Chivers said.

'And what did that consist of other than the fact you

had arrested and charged him and he denied his guilt!'

'Anyway, what's so special about your clients?' Chivers asked belligerently.

Robin Snaith grinned. 'Nothing, except they are *my* clients.'

Brian, who had listened to this exchange with absorbed interest, notched up yet another point in his solicitor's favour. Not even the return journey to Brixton prison at the end of the day was able to reduce him to his state of erstwhile dejection.

With Mr Snaith, assisted by Rosa Epton, looking after his interests, he felt he was bound to be acquitted.

CHAPTER SEVENTEEN

Two days later, the trial of Gregor Maltby and three other men opened at the Old Bailey.

Security precautions were especially stringent in the light of possible trouble by sympathisers with the accused. Extra police manned the doors into court and no one was admitted until his credentials had been established.

Those trying to get into the public gallery were scrutinised as though they might be carriers of plague, particularly anyone who from his appearance—and such weren't difficult to detect—might be friendly towards the prisoners in the dock.

If the police on duty could have had their way, sympathisers would have been barred from the court-room, but, as they'd been among the first in the queue, they had to be allowed in. Moreover, they were ready to assert their right of entry as was evidenced by the several altercations which took place between them and the officers on the door.

Though Mr Justice Pearn had not received any further threats, no chances were being taken with regard to his safety and, for the past ten days, a constable had never strayed far from the front-door of his home and his arrival at the Old Bailey had been the subject of further precautions.

Arnold Feely, who was defending a man named Struthers, was known to the officer guarding the entrance into court and was admitted without difficulty. He took his seat and awaited the four knocks on the door which would herald the judge's appearance on the bench. He slipped the piece of pink tape off his brief and twisted it nervously round his index finger. The clerk from his instructing solicitors glanced at him and came to the conclusion that he'd had a heavy night and not much sleep. Feely discarded the tape and began fiddling with a pencil. The truth was that he was feeling as ill-at-ease as he appeared, though the cause had nothing to do with the trial which was about to start.

His wife had left for Brussels the previous day and he was now certain that Detective Sergeant Craddock had gone with her. After she had departed, he had tried to phone Craddock and been told that he was on leave for the next three days, which had confirmed his suspicion. He had not, as his solicitor's clerk suspected, been out drinking the night before, though he had lain awake for a large part of it, trying to make up his mind what to do about the situation. Up until a few days ago, he'd believed he was in control of it, but now he was less sure. It was how to regain that control which now occupied his mind.

The knocks on the bench door interrupted his thoughts and he stood up as Mr Justice Pearn made his entry.

There followed the ritual exchange of bows and then everyone sat down again.

A minute later the four accused came into the dock and there was a small burst of clapping from the public gallery. Maltby glanced up and waved in that direction. An usher shouted for silence and a police officer laid an itching hand on the collar of one of the demonstrators. At this point Mr Justice Pearn spoke.

'Should there be any further outbursts of that nature, the court will be immediately cleared and will remain so for the duration of the trial.'

Everyone looked suitably solemn save for the demonstrators and the accused who grinned amongst themselves. After they had all pleaded not guilty, the jury was empanelled. This occupied a considerable amount of time as jurors found themselves challenged on behalf of one accused or another and were picked off like silhouettes on top of a wall. As each departed with an expression of bafflement or relief he was replaced by another.

Eventually, even Gregor Maltby who was defending himself seemed to tire of the exercise and the jury was duly sworn.

By the time the lunch adjournment was reached, leading counsel appearing for the prosecution was only half-way through his opening speech, which went on to occupy most of the afternoon as well. If it achieved little else, it certainly had the effect of defusing the highly charged atmosphere in which the trial had begun. Only Maltby himself appeared to give it his undivided attention as he sat forward listening intently and making copious notes.

It seemed almost an anti-climax when the court rose again just after four o'clock without further dramatic interruption.

It was while Mr Justice Pearn was disrobing that his clerk entered and told him that a young man in the public gallery had been in possession of a stink bomb.

'How does anyone know?' the judge enquired.

'It went off in his pocket as he was leaving court.'

'That seems penalty enough,' the judge observed dryly.

'And they won't let him back in tomorrow, of course.'

'That seems right and proper, too.'

'I doubt whether we'll get any trouble, sir. The police seem to have taken every possible precaution to prevent anything happening.'

'I doubt it, too. It's usually all anonymous boast and bombast from a safe distance, but one can never take chances.' He picked up his bowler hat and umbrella. 'Well, I'm going off to my club. I'll see you in the morning.'

As he made his way out of the building, he reflected on the Old Bailey as he'd first known it. The marble halls, the grandiose waste of space and only four courts. Now, there had been grafted on to this a modern functional building containing over a dozen new courts and a complex of corridors. Those behind the public scene were richly carpeted, which was no solace to him when he found himself alone in one of them and lost. I could be assassinated right here in the building, he reflected sardonically, and probably no one would know until I was found by a cleaner tomorrow morning.

He arrived at the Blackstone to discover Talbot doing door duty.

'What's happened to the usual man?' he enquired, after a friendly greeting to Talbot.

'He just hasn't been in today. It seems you can't rely on anyone these days,' Talbot said with a contemptuous sniff. 'First young Tanner and now this man.'

'Yes, most unfortunate about Tanner,' Sir John Pearn said briskly, 'but obviously these things can happen in the best ordered houses.'

'Quite so, Sir John, but the young are so inconsiderate. No sense of dignity or responsibility. I see from the evening paper that they tried to cause trouble in your court today.'

'Only a minor eruption. It was soon dealt with and there was no repetition. Probably realised they'd end up inside if they got too frisky. Contempt of court, you know.'

'If you ask me, we ought to deal with them much more severely. It's because we've been so weak-kneed that they take all these advantages. The country could do without them.'

'Like to see the death penalty brought back, would you, Talbot?'

'I would, Sir John. And the birch!'

Sir John Pearn smiled. 'I'll be up in the bar if I'm wanted,' he said, turning on his heel.

'Just a moment, sir. I believe I saw something here for you.'

Talbot scanned the ledge on which members' mail awaited collection.

'Yes, I thought so.' He picked up a small brown paper package and handed it to the judge. It was addressed to: Sir John Pearn, Chairman of the Blackstone Club, Iberia Street, W.C.2.

He turned it over, gave it a small shake and then put it in his pocket.

'Looks like someone has sent you a piece of wedding cake,' Talbot said archly.

'Who? Any member of the staff got married recently?'

'No.'

'It's probably a sample of some sort. I'm always being sent them.'

The only other person in the bar when he arrived there was Arnold Feely. As he entered, he noticed him toss back the drink he had in his hand with a compulsiveness that caused Sir John to frown. What was he doing drinking like that at this early hour of the evening! Even as he noted it, Sir John decided to retreat. He didn't want to get involved drinking with Arnold Feely of all people. Unfortunately, Feely looked round at that moment.

'Hello, judge,' he said heartily, 'let me buy you a drink.'

'That's very kind of you, Feely,' Sir John said unenthusiastically. 'I'll have a small Scotch.'

'A large Scotch for Sir John,' Feely said to the barman.

'A small one,' the judge added firmly. He lifted his glass. 'Here's to you.'

'And to you, judge. I don't think we need toast those in the dock at the Old Bailey.' Feely had intended this to come out as a humorous aside, but, even as he spoke, he realised it didn't sound funny. This was confirmed by the judge's expression.

The judge swallowed his drink in one. 'Excuse me if I don't return the compliment just now, but I have business to transact with the secretary.'

Left alone once more, Arnold Feely ordered himself another large Scotch. The barman poured it for him and went back to reading his paper in the corner, while Feely stared morosely at the row of bottles on the Dutch dresser which formed the back of the bar. Life was a mess and he wasn't sure that all the whisky in the Blackstone was going to help make it less so.

Colonel Tatham jumped to his feet when Sir John Pearn came into his office.

'Don't get up, Tatham. Apologise for disturbing you, but I'm trying to avoid certain company in the bar. Tell me, have you noticed Feely overdoing the drinking a bit recently?'

The secretary frowned thoughtfully. 'Can't say I have. I always feel a bit sorry for him.'

'Sorry for him!' Sir John's tone was sharp. 'Why's that?'

'He always impresses me as someone who would like to get on better with people than he does. I think he may sometimes feel that he's not completely accepted by his fellow members.'

'He might do better if he didn't try so hard to be liked! Anyway, I'm glad you don't think he's drinking too much. It's a bad reputation to get at the Bar and, though it may be beneficial to the club's profits, it's not something we want to encourage here.' He glanced round the small cluttered room. 'We really ought to provide our secretary with somewhere better to work.'

'This is perfectly adequate. It's not as though I'm immured here all day.'

'Even so . . .' He let the sentence tail away. 'Heard anything further from the police?'

Colonel Tatham shook his head. 'Not a word. I think the bequests sub-committee ought to consider the matter at its next meeting. Leaving the display cases empty is an unhappy reminder of our loss and it doesn't look as if we'll get the snuff-boxes back. At least, I personally don't think we shall.'

'I agree. Even if the police ever catch the culprits, it's unlikely they'll still have the property.' He paused and frowned. 'A thoroughly nasty business!' he remarked. 'Not least the distasteful suggestion that someone in the club connived at the theft.'

'It's inconceivable.'

'I would like to believe so. The police haven't pursued that aspect further with you?'

'Not since I informed Chief Superintendent Samson, after he'd asked us to consider the possibility, that we were unable to endorse it as a profitable line of investigation.'

'I like the way you put that,' Sir John Pearn remarked, with a smile. 'Have they taken the heat off old Talbot now?'

'I don't think he's under suspicion any longer, though the mystery of the keys remains. One has to conclude that the thief used Talbot's bunch to unlock and then re-lock the display cases.'

'The old boy probably sleeps like a log. And I've always

thought how easy it would be for someone to slip into the club just before it closes, when it's virtually empty, and then hide.'

'Less easy now as a result of our new precautions.'

'We're great ones for locking stable doors after the horses have bolted!'

'That was certainly true in the army.'

While they'd been talking, Sir John Pearn had produced the small brown-paper package from his pocket and had begun opening it. Wrestling with the strip of Sellotape which went right round it, he said:

'I know of nothing quite so maddening as trying to unwrap something these days. Things are done up as if one isn't intended to get at the contents.'

'Shall I have a try?'

'No, it's all right, I think I'm winning.'

With a final tug, he ripped off the outer covering of paper and threw it down on the floor. He was left with a small object wrapped in corrugated cardboard which was held round it by more bands of Sellotape. The further wrapping did not, however, cover the two ends of the object inside and Sir John held one end up to his eye before embarking on a final battle to reveal the contents.

Colonel Tatham saw his expression become one of astonishment.

'Good lord! What's that look like to you?' he asked, passing the object to the secretary.

'A small box of some sort.'

'It's a snuff-box!'

He seized it back and tore off the remaining wrapping.

The next second there was a hissing sound, accompanied by a bright flash and a large amount of smoke and Sir John Pearn let out an unjudicial yelp as he dropped the object on to the floor.

Colonel Tatham sprang to his feet and, seizing a carafe of water, poured it where the thing had fallen.

'Are you all right, Sir John?'

'I think so. My hand's a bit burnt, but otherwise no damage.' He glanced down at the snuff-box. 'It must have been booby-trapped,' he said in an outraged tone. 'You'd better get on to the police right away. Meanwhile, not a word to anyone. We'll wait in here till the police come.'

Later when they learnt that Detective Chief Superintendent Samson would be round immediately, Colonel Tatham went into the bar to fetch a couple of large whiskies.

It was now fairly full and he chose a quiet end away from the crowd to make his purchase.

'What've you done to your face, secretary?' someone called out cheerfully.

'My face? Nothing, what's wrong with it?'

'Looks as though you've been making up for the minstrel show.'

Colonel Tatham gave the speaker a knowing smile, but refrained from comment until he could examine his countenance himself. On the way back to his office, he popped into the service lavatory on that floor which was part broom cupboard. It had a small mirror on the wall.

His left upper cheek and the side of his nose were covered in blackish powder. He touched the area with the tip of his finger which, in turn, became black.

A minute later he emerged, having wiped his face clean. As far as he was concerned, the police would have to be satisfied with secondary evidence of his appearance.

In the stunned surprise which had followed the incident, he had failed to notice Sir John's appearance, but he now looked at him covertly as he returned with the drinks. His face was considerably blacker and it also appeared that one of his eyebrows had been singed.

'I phoned my doctor while you were out of the room,' the judge said. 'My left hand is distinctly painful and I think it had better be attended to as soon as possible. I

148

also seem to be smothered in black powder, but I thought I'd let that be until Samson has come and seen for himself the effect of the device which went off.'

Colonel Tatham nodded gravely. It was almost as if the judge was intent on preserving himself as exhibit one.

When, shortly afterwards, Samson arrived, he didn't reveal his emotions by so much as a flicker of an eyelid. It was as if he was used to seeing Her Majesty's judges under every sort of condition.

Nursing his left hand in his lap, Sir John Pearn described what had happened while Samson and the officer he'd brought with him listened attentively. When the judge had finished, Samson gathered up the wrapping off the floor and laid the various fragments of paper on the secretary's desk. Lastly, he picked up the snuff-box, whose lid had been wrenched back by the explosion, and sniffed the interior.

'Are you able to say, sir, whether this was one of the snuff-boxes which was stolen?'

'It's one that was recently presented to the club by Miss Beresford, whose deceased brother used to be a member of the club. Despite the damage, I can identify it by the silver mount. And you can see the mother of pearl under the muck that's now on it. It's definitely one of ours. One of our members was against our accepting it and so I had occasion to examine it more closely than I would otherwise, in order to form a judgment.'

'Why was this member against the club accepting it?' Samson enquired.

'Didn't think it worthy to go into our collection.'

'May I ask who the member was?'

'I suppose so. Not that he'd have had anything to do with this outrage. It was ex-Judge Whitby-Stansford.'

'I see,' Samson said, with a thoughtful expression. A second later, he picked up the pieces of wrapping paper which bore the judge's name and the club's address. 'Do you recognise this writing by any chance, sir?'

'No.'

'I know it's always difficult with printed capitals, but some people do make certain letters distinctively.'

'I'm afraid I can't assist. Anyway, it's hardly likely to have been sent by anyone I know personally.'

Samson nodded. 'Well, sir, we'll have all these items examined at the laboratory. They'll be able to tell us what caused the thing to explode. Seems to me it may have been intended to go off rather more violently than it did.'

'It did go off a bit like a bad firework,' the secretary agreed.

'It went off like an extremely effective firework,' the judge said with a strong note of judicial frost in his voice.

CHAPTER EIGHTEEN

Mr Justice Pearn was trying the Maltby case. Mr Justice Pearn had received a letter warning him not to be the trial judge. The warning had been ignored and now he had been sent an exploding snuff-box. Mr Justice Pearn was also the chairman of the Blackstone Club from which the snuff-box in question had been stolen. A young man named Brian Tanner had been employed at the Blackstone. Brian Tanner now stood charged with the murder of Harry Green, a known thief and small-time informant.

These were just some of the pieces of puzzle with which Samson, Chivers and the officer in charge of the Maltby case were confronted when they conferred at Scotland

Yard under the chairmanship of a Deputy Assistant Commissioner.

The trouble was that the pieces didn't all seem to belong to the same puzzle. It was as if a child had been playing with three jig-saws at once and had got the pieces mixed when he returned them to their boxes.

And yet the combined instinct of these experienced officers told them that there must be a connecting thread between these disparate events.

'I gather the judge doesn't intend adjourning the Maltby trial?' the D.A.C. said, looking towards Samson.

'He made that quite clear, sir,' Samson replied. 'His doctor wanted him to go home and rest for a couple of days, but his lordship wouldn't hear of it. Told him he had a duty to perform and he was perfectly well able to try a case with one arm in a sling and that the public interest overrode any considerations of personal comfort.'

'What did the doctor say to all that?' the D.A.C. enquired with an amused expression.

'He just shrugged and said something about being as used to having his advice disregarded as must be the judge.'

'The nub of the problem, as I see it,' the D.A.C. said after a pause, 'is whether the explosive snuff-box was sent to him as judge in the Maltby trial or as Sir John Pearn, chairman of the Blackstone Club. I know it was addressed to him at the club, but I think that was because whoever sent it realised it would be the best way of ensuring he'd open it himself. If it had been sent to him at the Old Bailey, it would have been examined before it ever reached him. So the fact that it was posted to the Blackstone and addressed to Sir John Pearn, rather than Mr Justice Pearn, does not, in my view, help us one way or the other.'

'Why should anyone want to harm him in his capacity as chairman of the Blackstone Club?' Samson asked.

'Why, indeed!'

'In my view, it was obviously sent by some of Maltby's sympathisers,' the officer in charge of that case said. 'It's just the sort of thing they'd do.'

'Are you suggesting then that it was Maltby's sympathisers who were behind the theft of the snuff-boxes from the Blackstone?' the D.A.C. asked. 'Because that wouldn't seem to be their normal line of activity.'

'I wonder if these events really are connected,' Samson said thoughtfully. 'I still think it's possible that some old crank took the snuff-boxes. Or rather, that they were stolen on his behalf.'

'Why should he send one of them back booby-trapped?'

'Simply because he is a cranky old man.'

'Do you have someone in mind who fits the bill?'

Samson nodded. 'An old boy called Whitby-Stansford. He's a retired circuit judge and a member of the Blackstone. He lives alone in a large house up on Campden Hill, which is stuffed with valuable pieces. He's well known in the antique world as a buyer *and* a seller. And he also has the reputation of being a bit of a crank. He doesn't like being crossed and has been known to react really nastily when he's been thwarted.'

'You've obviously made quite a study of him,' the D.A.C. said quietly.

'Yes, I have. I managed to get someone inside his house, too.'

'But no snuff-boxes there?'

'No, none *there*. But I have reason to believe he hoards stuff somewhere else and I'm still trying to find out where.'

'I'm still not clear,' the D.A.C. said, 'why he should have sent this one snuff-box back filled with explosive or whatever it was. Cranky he may be, but that seems to me to be carrying crankiness into a different realm altogether.'

'Let me try and explain, sir. This particular snuff-box had recently been presented to the club by the sister of a deceased member who had owned it. It seems that old Whitby-Stansford thought it a trashy item and told the committee they should reject the offer. But they didn't. So, given that he's a crank, who doesn't like being crossed, he now has a motive for doing what he did. And isn't it just the sort of thing a crank of his kidney might do? It would fill him with a sense of poetic justice.'

'But to pack it with explosive...' The D.A.C.'s tone showed that he was unpersuaded.

'I'm pretty sure it wasn't explosive, sir. I think it was black powder. The stuff you get in fireworks. It flares up when ignited, but it doesn't explode. The lab will soon let us know if I'm right. If I am, it's fairly clear that someone's intention was not to kill the judge, probably not even to cause him serious injury, but merely to give him a fright.'

'And you seriously believe the someone could be Judge Whitby-Stansford?'

Samson glanced round the faces of his case-hardened colleagues. He couldn't blame them for looking so disbelieving of the theory he'd just propounded. On the other hand, it was his investigation and not theirs and he proposed to go on pursuing his own line of enquiry. He felt pretty certain that Brian and Harry Green were involved in the burglary and it was to proving their link with the old ex-judge that he determined to bend his efforts anew. It wasn't sufficient that Brian and Whitby-Stansford would have come into contact through the Blackstone. He had to prove something closer and more positive than that. His glance came back to the D.A.C.

'I think it's a possibility, sir, which merits further investigation,' he said in a more detached tone than he'd used when advancing his theory.

'O.K., Sam, don't let our doubts head you off. But, meanwhile, we must consider the other possibilities...'

*   *   *

For several days now, Detective Constable Denny had been keeping a discreet watch on ex-Judge Whitby-Stansford's house in Kensington. It was in a quiet street which ran near the top of Campden Hill which made observation difficult without arousing suspicion. It had long been a good catchment area for burglaries and householders were liable to phone the police if they saw anyone obviously loitering in the area.

D.C. Denny had so far managed to avoid the embarrassment of becoming the subject of such a call, but only by maintaining a less continuous watch than he deemed satisfactory.

Each time the ex-judge left the house, his instructions were to follow him. Their morning journeys invariably ended at the Blackstone Club. Luckily, the old boy had an aversion to taxis, or was too mean to take one, and travelled by public transport which made surveillance much easier.

On two occasions, however, he had not gone direct to the club, but had, on one, visited an antique shop in Church Street and, on another, gone to an exhibition of Georgian silver in Bond Street. But so far he had not led Denny to the secret storage room which Detective Chief Superintendent Samson believed him to own.

On the morning after the conference at Scotland Yard, Denny was trying to look inconspicuous as he hung about at the end of the judge's road. There was a smell of early spring in the air and, if one had to be doing what he was, it was as pleasant a day for it as any. The tree under which he was standing had burgeoned overnight, it seemed, which caused him to wonder if he'd still be there when its leaves began to fall. Such had become the ennui of his vigil.

He saw the judge's front-door open and the owner emerge, double-locking it carefully behind him. This was the hour he usually came out and headed for Notting Hill underground station from which he would travel to

Holborn where he would alight and set off on a ten minutes' walk to the Blackstone.

Denny suddenly noticed with a quickening of interest that he was carrying a canvas holdall, which was something he'd not seen him do previously. It gave the appearance of being empty. Also it was soon clear that he was not making for Notting Hill station. Instead, he turned into Church Street and walked briskly in the direction of Kensington High Street. When he reached the main road, he turned left and walked almost as far as the Albert Hall before crossing the road and heading south.

After a couple more turns, during which Denny closed up on him, they arrived in a cobblestone mews of small expensive flats above the rows of lock-up garages which lined either side.

By now, Denny was sure that Samson's belief was about to be confirmed.

The mews appeared to be deserted apart from a small boy kicking a football against one of the garage doors at the further end. Denny realised that if he entered the mews, he would almost certainly attract the old man's attention, even though he'd given the impression of being wholly oblivious of anything going on around him. In any event, it wasn't necessary to go further in order to see where he went.

As Denny was still assessing the situation, ex-Judge Whitby-Stansford suddenly veered across to a garage door on the left and paused in front of it while he unbuttoned his top-coat and put a hand into an inner pocket. He appeared to have trouble in finding the right key, but then he unlocked a wicket in the main garage door and stepped inside. A moment later the wicket was pulled to and only the boy with a football remained as evidence of life in the mews.

Denny decided to walk past the door through which ex-Judge Whitby-Stansford had disappeared. When he reached it, he saw it was number 18 and that it was one in need of repainting. Most were so bright and spruce-looking that they made the others look drab by contrast. The door of number 18 had once been pea green in colour, but was now faded and peeling.

Denny cast his eyes up at the living quarters above. There were clean lace curtains over the windows and the flat was plainly occupied, presumably let separate from the garage.

He walked on until he reached the boy, who was still kicking his football indefatigably against a door as much in need of a coat of paint as the one he'd just been looking at.

'Hello,' he said.

'Hello,' the boy said, without looking round.

He waited until the ball bounced near him and then fielded it.

'Do you live here?'

The boy nodded.

'Not at number eighteen?' The boy shook his head. 'Do you know who does live there?' Again the boy shook his head. 'What's your name?' The boy stared meaningly at the football, but made no reply. 'Which do you live in?'

By this time the boy had become red in the face and looked as though he might be about to cry.

'I'm sorry,' Denny said, rolling the football back to him, 'I just thought you might be able to help me.'

'My name's Richard and I'm not allowed to talk to strangers,' the boy said accusingly as he picked up the ball and made to run off.

Denny sighed. First, he'd risked being reported for loitering with intent and now for importuning small boys for an immoral purpose. Such were the hazards when keeping one retired judge under observation.

He turned round intending to retrace his steps when

the wicket of number 18 suddenly opened and ex-Judge Whitby-Stansford stepped through. At the same moment as Denny noticed that the old man was no longer carrying the holdall, he also realised that he was heading in his direction. There was nothing for it, but to pretend he was walking the other way.

As they passed, however, the judge didn't accord him so much as a flickering glance.

Denny quickened his step as he made for the nearest public telephone to report his news to Detective Chief Superintendent Samson.

CHAPTER NINETEEN

'Trouble about these short flights is they don't allow enough drinking-time,' Detective Sergeant Craddock said, as he downed his third Scotch while the stewardess stood waiting to remove his glass.

In a few minutes the plane would be landing at Heathrow after its forty minutes' flight from Brussels. It had only been by intimidation that he had managed to get a third drink at all. The plane was full and the cabin staff had been kept more than busy throughout the flight, and the stewardess in question had soon noted Craddock as the sort of demanding and trouble-making passenger she could happily do without.

Next to him Marcia Feely fastened her seat-belt and gave him a small, tired smile.

'We'll fly over the Pole to Japan sometime,' she said, 'that'll give you longer.'

He grinned. 'Better go separately through Customs and Immigration,' he said. 'It's always possible one of the Special Branch officers may know me and we don't want to excite any comment.'

She nodded. 'Whichever of us gets through first can wait outside.'

'Is Arnold likely to be at the flat when you get there?'

'I've no idea. I said I'd probably get back this evening, but that was all.'

'You didn't phone him from Brussels?'

'No.' She glanced out of the window as they skimmed over the M.4 on their approach to landing. She was frowning when she turned back. 'I have a feeling Arnold's going to be difficult.'

'About this trip you mean? How can he be? He doesn't know I went over with you, does he?'

'No, he doesn't, and I don't mean about this trip in particular, but about things in general.'

'He's in no position to be difficult,' Craddock said brusquely.

'I hope that's so.'

'Of course it is. He'll be committing professional suicide if he gets out of step and he knows it.' His tone was grim as he went on, 'If he does show any sign of getting stroppy, one small twist of his balls will soon bring him back into line.'

'Basically, he's a weak man and that's the danger.'

'Weak men are frightened men.'

'That's what worries me.'

'In his case, fright will operate to make him keep his mouth shut. He daren't do otherwise.'

'Let's hope so.'

'I do more than hope, I know.'

The plane, which had landed, was now taxiing up to the terminal building, after what seemed like circuiting the whole airport.

'We could easily have had another drink,' Craddock observed.

'The bar's closed.'

'I know it is, but we've spent almost as long scurrying about runways as we did in the air.'

Marcia cast him a sidelong look of appraisal. He was as tough and self-reliant as they came and good-looking, too, in an utterly masculine way. She had once asked him why he hadn't got further in the police and he'd said that his divorce hadn't helped him and that, anyway, there were always some whose faces didn't fit. It was then she had said that his face fitted very nicely with her. And that had really been the start of it all.

The only thing about him she didn't like was his name, Sid. When they were alone, she usually called him Tony because, as she said, he looked like a Tony to her. Tonys were tough, handsome and virile, with a dash of ruthlessness thrown in. But when she spoke of him to Arnold, it was always Sid, though she always gave a small shiver of revulsion every time she used the name.

The plane came to a halt and the doors were opened and Marcia experienced the faint feeling of dread that usually overcame her at this moment of return. Euphoria evaporated as the plane reached a conclusive halt. Adventure was over—and, after all, every trip abroad was an adventure—and the routine of everyday life waited to envelop one again. Her thoughts were interrupted by Craddock who leaned over her to retrieve his briefcase.

'A successful trip, I think, don't you?' he murmured with one eyebrow cocked to give him a mischievous expression.

She nodded. 'Yes, Tony. A very successful one. In every way.'

CHAPTER TWENTY

When Detective Chief Superintendent Samson brought up the question of applying for a search warrant under the Theft Act to search ex-Judge Whitby-Stansford's mews garage, his Deputy Assistant Commissioner stared at him and then said pleasantly:

'Are you out of your mind, Sam?'

'You don't think it's on, sir?'

'Not until you have a reasonable belief he's storing stolen property there. Reasonable being the operative word.'

'We've obtained search warrants on less.' Samson's tone had a note of plea.

'Not on my authority. And not against judges.'

'Would there be any objection to my interviewing him?'

'None, provided you go about it tactfully.'

'Oh, I'll do that all right.'

'Go ahead, then.'

And so it was that the next morning found Samson on the doorstep of the judge's home keeping a ten o'clock appointment.

He was let in by a woman in an overall and shown into the drawing-room on the first floor. He had hardly had time to survey his surroundings before ex-Judge Whitby-Stansford entered.

'Good morning, officer,' he said, as he went and sat down, 'now what is it you want to see me about? Sit down if you wish.'

Samson sat down on a chair facing the ex-judge.

'It's about the theft of the Blackstone's snuff-boxes, sir.'

'Found them, have you?'

'No, sir.'

'Doubt if you ever will.'

'Of course one of them was sent to Sir John Pearn...'

'Yes, shocking business,' ex-Judge Whitby-Stansford broke in. 'Don't know what the country's coming to when Her Majesty's judges can be subjected to such outrages!'

'I gather the snuff-box which blew up,' Samson went on stolidly, 'had been the object of some controversy.'

'Don't quite know what you mean by that.'

'Some members, yourself amongst them, had been against accepting it for the club's collection.'

'As far as I know I was the only person who spoke up to that effect.'

'But the committee felt otherwise.'

'What are you getting at?' the ex-judge asked in a fierce tone.

'Nothing, sir.'

'You're not trying to suggest that I had anything to do with this business?'

'Of course not, sir, but I'd be interested to hear any theories you may hold.'

'Why should I, in particular, have any theories?'

'I gather you're quite a collector yourself, sir. It therefore occurred to me you might have some ideas as to the disposal of the snuff-boxes.'

'I would have hoped it might also have occurred to you that, as a responsible citizen, I should have informed the police of anything useful to them within my knowledge.'

'Very often people don't like taking that sort of initiative, sir.'

'And so you've called to see me?'

'Yes, sir.'

'Why didn't you come sooner then?' The question shot out like a pointing finger.

Samson blinked at its suddenness.

'Solely because our first line of enquiry having failed to produce results, sir, we're now widening the scope of the investigation.'

It was a reply with which he felt rather pleased, but he still wondered why the old man was behaving with such aggressive suspicion. Was it because he had something to hide? Or simply because he was a cranky old boy?

'Well, I can't help you,' ex-Judge Whitby-Stansford said with an air of finality.

Samson glanced about the room. Over against the far wall stood two glass-fronted cabinets which were full of small objects, presumably valuable, but which he was unable to see properly from where he was sitting. In any event, it was extremely unlikely that he would find the Blackstone's collection of snuff-boxes in either. If they ever had been there, his telephone call the day before would have been sufficient to ensure their removal.

The interview had run its course and got him nowhere. It was even possible that the ex-judge would make an official complaint about the questions he'd been asked, though Samson felt confident that, if he did, he would receive a courteous but unyielding reply. Not that you could be certain of anything these days. Any old member of the public could make any old sort of allegation against a police officer and the law required it to be solemnly recorded and investigated. It often seemed to Samson that half the force spent its time enquiring into the alleged misdeeds of the other half—to no one's satisfaction.

He got up from his chair and ex-Judge Whitby-Stansford did likewise.

'It doesn't look, sir, as if you have much room for anything more. But I imagine that's a problem which all collectors face. What to do when the space runs out?'

For a few seconds the old man stared at him with an expression of cold dislike.

'It has been clear to me from the outset, officer, that you have come here on a snooping expedition. I can only suppose that some malicious person has put suggestions into your mind, which you felt it necessary to explore. I have not enjoyed your visit and, as I am unable to afford you any assistance at all in connection with your enquiries, I shall be obliged if you will now leave.'

'I'm sorry, sir, if I've given you offence, but I've only been doing my duty as I see it.'

Ex-Judge Whitby-Stansford brushed past him while he was speaking and flung open the door.

'Mrs Potter,' he called out, 'will you kindly show this person to the front door.'

Samson's car was waiting outside and he got in beside the driver, mopping his brow as he did so.

'Where to, sir?'

'The Yard.' They had set off when he added, 'Go via Hall Mews. I want to take a look at number eighteen.'

When they arrived there, he got out of the car and gave the garage doors a close scrutiny.

One thing he noticed, which D.C. Denny hadn't mentioned, was that they were fitted with a burglar alarm.

For the rest of the journey, he was wrapped in silent thought. One way or another he was more than ever determined to have a look inside the garage of number 18.

CHAPTER TWENTY-ONE

A few days later the statements of evidence which formed the basis of the prosecution's case against Brian were sent to his solicitor and the same day Rosa Epton put them in her briefcase and set out for Brixton prison.

Brian was delighted to see her and immediately forgot how low-spirited he had been feeling. They met in the same interview room as before. Rosa was wearing a fluffy wool skirt of deep purple and a black turtle-neck sweater. On a chain round her neck hung a small gold medallion.

Brian thought she looked terrific.

'It might be easier if you brought your chair round and sat beside me,' she said matter-of-factly, 'and then we can go through the statements together.' She laid the bundle on the table where they could both look at them. 'I have read them already and so has Mr Snaith.' Brian glanced at her enquiringly. 'But it's your reactions we want.'

'Do you think I'll be acquitted?'

'I think that largely depends on one witness—or perhaps I should say two.'

'Which two?'

'The man called George Pratt who says he saw you leaving the scene of the crime—and yourself.'

'Me?' He glanced at her with a puzzled expression.

'In the final analysis the jury are going to have to decide whether they believe Pratt or you.'

'But that's not fair! I thought the prosecution had to prove its case, not just ask the jury to toss a coin between me and one of their witnesses.'

'I'm afraid I over-simplified the issue which is always a dangerous thing to do. I forgot, for a moment, that you'd had previous experience of trials.'

'Acquitted each time, mind you!'

'I hadn't forgotten that,' she said with one of her fleeting smiles. 'The position is, of course, that if the jury isn't satisfied with Pratt's evidence, if they think he may be mistaken, then the case against you will have been seriously undermined.'

'He is mistaken,' Brian said emphatically. He wanted

to tell Rosa that Pratt was more than mistaken, he was a lying witness. But this he couldn't do. The trouble was that, even if he did decide to tell her the whole truth, his theory about being framed sounded utterly implausible when he couldn't begin to suggest who it was who had framed him. No, he was lumbered with what he'd told the police and he'd have to stick with it. There was nothing more certain to attract a judge's acid comments than a defendant's change of story.

'Let's look at his statement first,' Rosa said, turning pages of the bundle. 'This is it.'

Brian could feel the warmth of her body as he drew his chair in closer and focused his attention on the statement she had turned to.

'Statement of George Pratt of 126 Capon Street, N.1 ... self-employed ... who saith as follows: At about 2015 hours on 6th March, I was walking along Hersholt Street after leaving the Plumbers Arms Public House where I had gone to meet an acquaintance who had not turned up. I was just about opposite number 42 Hersholt Street on the other side of the road when a young chap, whom I later picked out on an identification parade as the accused, came bursting out of the front door. He paused on the pavement for a moment and glanced both ways before running off in the Euston direction. I immediately went and dialled 999. I have no doubt that the person I picked out on the identification parade is the same person I saw running away from number 42 Hersholt Street.'

There followed a certificate to the effect that the statement was true to the best of his knowledge and belief and that George Pratt realised he'd be for the high jump if it was ever proved otherwise.

Rosa was watching him as he finished reading the statement. 'Well?' she said, in a quietly coaxing tone.

'How could he have seen me when I was never there?'

'He's very definite about it.'

Brian nodded glumly. Talk about dilemmas with horns. He was really impaled. He knew quite well there'd been no one standing on the opposite pavement when he emerged from number 42. And even if there had been, he'd certainly never have been able to recognise Brian from the fleeting glimpse he'd have had of him. Far from pausing and glancing both ways before showing his heels, his flight from the house had been one rapid, continuing movement—and in an ill-lit street at that.

'The chap who did murder Green must have resembled me,' he said, unhappily.

'Your double, perhaps?'

'I'm not saying that,' he said, stung by her tone.

'I'm glad. Doubles went out with what my father used to call the soldier's defence. He did a lot of court martial work when he was in the army and he always said that soldiers had a wonderful way of remembering clearly any detail in their favour, but of claiming amnesia in respect of what they were alleged to have done. If they weren't suffering from amnesia, they'd usually say that the crime must have been committed by their double.'

Brian felt that the smile he gave her probably appeared rather sickly. He didn't enjoy being on the receiving end of her ridicule. He preferred to think of them preparing his defence in eager partnership.

'Whoever it was doesn't need to have been my double for Pratt to be mistaken.'

'That's true, but what we have to meet—and overcome if you're going to be acquitted—is the fact that he subsequently picked you out, apparently without difficulty, at a properly conducted identification parade.'

Brian nodded gloomily. Rosa, for her part, decided not to tell him that she thought George Pratt was open to some effective cross-examination as a result of her own investigations. There was no point in sustaining him with what might prove to be false hopes. It was better to let her head rule her heart, which was the way she always tried to keep it in her work.

'Let's go through the rest of the statements,' she said. 'Now, this man, Riccardi, who owns the café where you met the person you knew as Stan, but who obviously was Harry Green, I take it there's nothing you disagree with in what he says?'

Brian read the statement in question intently. 'He makes it appear as though we were hatching a plot when he says "they were talking seriously together and in low voices". We were just chatting over a cup of tea.'

Rosa nodded and made a note in her book. 'Have a look through the police evidence.' When Brian had finished reading, she said, 'Any comments?'

'I don't think so. At least, they haven't put in any verbals.'

'They don't always,' she remarked.

'How do you and Mr Snaith feel about the evidence?' he asked, a trifle nervously.

'Provided we can make a dent in Pratt, I think Mr Snaith feels you've got a sporting chance.'

'And you, what do you think?'

'I'm merely Mr Snaith's assistant, I don't have views on his clients' cases,' she said, giving him one of her small attractive smiles.

'But you must have private views.'

She shook her head. 'If I have, they remain private.'

'I'd love to know . . .'

'There are a couple of other things I wanted to mention,' she said, choosing to ignore his pleading look. 'First, I'd like to know where I can get hold of your girl-friend. I need to take a proof of evidence from her supporting what you told the police about the money they found being your savings.' She picked up her pen ready to write down the address.

'I'm afraid I can't tell you where she is,' he said lamely.

Rosa frowned. 'Can't or won't?'

'No, can't. That's honest, I don't know where she is.'

'She hasn't been to visit you?' Rosa's tone was one of surprise, but with a note of suspicion.

'No. I had a letter from her saying she couldn't come yet, but that she'd be in touch as soon as various things were settled.'

Rosa pursed her lips. 'Was there no address on the letter?'

'No.'

'And you have no idea where I can get hold of her?'

'I'm afraid not.'

'I see,' she said in the voice of someone suddenly filled with pregnant thoughts.

'Fiona has problems of her own,' he said desperately. 'I know she will get in touch with me as soon as she can. She'll never let me down.'

'I hope she doesn't leave things too late,' Rosa observed with a faint note of asperity. She was beginning to wonder whether she ought to revise her original view of Brian. He had, she felt sure, been less than frank on a number of points. The question was, why?

'The other thing I wanted to mention isn't really relevant to your case. I take it you've been seeing newspapers while you've been here?'

'There isn't much else to do but read 'em.'

'Then you'll have read about this snuff-box which was sent to Mr Justice Pearn at the Blackstone Club and which exploded when he was opening the package which contained it?'

Brian passed his tongue across his lips which felt suddenly dry.

'Yeah, I read about it. He's a nice bloke, too, the judge. I'm glad he wasn't hurt badly.'

'And you realise, of course, that the police have been trying to link the theft of the snuff-boxes with the murder of Harry Green?'

'I should do! They questioned me enough about it.'

'I'm only asking this because one doesn't know exactly how things'll turn out in court and what mayn't suddenly be thrown up in evidence, but would you have any guesses about the mystery of the snuff-boxes? First, as to who took them and secondly, as to why one was sent back booby-trapped?'

'I don't know any more than I've told the police.'

'Anyway, just think about it,' she said, starting to put her papers back into her briefcase.

There was something in her tone which worried him. 'What is there I ought to think about?' he asked anxiously.

She paused in the act of fastening the catch on her briefcase and looked straight at him. 'Think about everything you've told the police and everything you've told me, of course. Never stop thinking. Your future is going to depend on it.'

'I don't understand what you're getting at.'

'I'm sure you do.' She rose.

'You're not going, are you?'

For the first time since he'd met her, she laughed.

'I'm afraid I must. I have to get back to the office and report to Mr Snaith.'

'Will you come again soon?'

'I'll see you at court in three days' time. That's when you'll be committed for trial. It'll just be a formality as we shall accept a committal on these statements without oral evidence being given. It's best to conserve our strength until we get to the Old Bailey. Then, it'll be into battle with colours flying.'

'Which barrister's going to defend me there?'

'Mr Snaith'll discuss that with you when he next sees you at court. I expect you'll have two. A Q.C. and a junior.' She reached the door and looked back at him standing forlorn as he watched her go. 'Good-bye,' she said, adding shyly, 'Brian.'

He was still smiling idiotically when the escorting officer took him back to the prison hospital.

As soon as Rosa reached the office, she went in to see Robin Snaith.

'Well, how did you find our client today?' he enquired lightly.

'I like him.'

'I know you do, but is he telling us the truth?'

'No.'

'Ha! So you like liars, do you, Miss Epton?' he barked in the mock tone of a hectoring cross-examiner.

She smiled. 'I'm certain he knows more than he's told us, but I don't think that his failure to be frank reflects his guilt.'

'You mayn't, but a jury, lacking your intuition, most probably will, if they ever fasten on the fact that he is hiding things.'

'I know.'

'Anyway, if he's not guilty, why can't he come clean?' She threw him a look and he went on, 'Yes, all right, that was a silly question! When one thinks of all the non-criminal reasons people have for not disclosing the truth or for not coming forward with vital information about some crime or other, it's surprising the wheels of justice manage to grind at all.' He stabbed at his blotting-pad with the point of a stiletto paper-knife. 'Presumably, you have some ideas about what he's hiding from us and why?'

'Nothing, really,' she said, slowly shaking her head. 'But there's something suspicious about this man, Pratt's, evidence. It's too pat, too positive. I just don't believe him.'

'If Tanner's to be believed, Pratt is either mistaken or he's a deliberate liar, who is all set to commit diabolical perjury. And we have absolutely no evidence whatsoever to suggest he's that.'

'That's just where I believe Brian could help us if he'd only tell the whole truth.'

'Help *himself*, you mean,' Smith said dryly. Privately, he registered with a touch of dismay the fact that this was the first time he had ever known Rosa to refer to a client by his first name. I hope to goodness she's not falling seriously for the guy, he thought. Perhaps, I'd better take her off the case.

'I think the truth may be that he's being framed, but can't say so,' she said, with a thoughtful expression.

'Well, just remember one thing,' Robin Snaith said in a resigned tone, 'it's sometimes embarrassing to know too much. It restricts one's freedom of action.'

'But other times surely it broadens it,' she replied with a flickering smile.

He sighed. 'Feminine intuition may be a splendid gift, but don't let it entirely replace all your other senses. Particularly, that labelled "common", which is certainly a criminal lawyer's strongest asset.'

'Don't worry. Just because I said I liked him and I've called him by his first name doesn't mean I've lost my head.'

Her principal stared at her in comical astonishment. Perhaps, he was wrong after all about the use of her intuitive sense. Particularly, as it wasn't the first time it had caused him to fall gracefully on his face.

'Would you like to hear about the rest of my interview with him?' she continued.

'Yes, go on,' he said, resolving firmly not to interrupt her any further.

CHAPTER TWENTY-TWO

In the days which followed a number of things happened, or failed to happen, that require little more than bare mention.

Brian was duly committed to stand his trial at the Old Bailey, the proceedings before the magistrate occupying less than a minute. Although he had been warned that it would be a foregone formality and although Mr Snaith was present and cheered him up afterwards by saying that Rosa Epton would be coming down to the prison to see him again about matters connected with his defence, he had found it a depressing day. Prison life while on remand was increasingly dispiriting, even to one who normally took each day as it came and was content to let the future look after itself. At times it seemed to him that he had never known any surroundings apart from the walls of Brixton prison. And now even his weekly outings to court had come to an end. His only consolation was being told that murder cases usually received some sort of priority in the jostling for a place in the trial lists.

Meanwhile, at the Old Bailey itself, the Maltby trial had become like a long distance race once the runners have settled down into the rhythm which is going to sustain them for endless laps. The defendants had made it clear that they were determined to challenge every comma of the prosecution's evidence and to spin out the trial for as long as they could. Mr Justice Pearn, who had discarded his sling and bandages after the first two days and now wore only a discreet dressing on his injured left hand, had decided, not without a degree of chafing reluctance, to give the defendants their head. He hoped that, by doing so, the jury would be impressed by his utter fairness, not to mention unimpressed by some of the captious, specious tactics of the defence. Since his receipt of the booby-trapped snuff-box, all security arrangements for the trial had become even more stringent. Compared with the other defending counsel in the case, Mr Justice Pearn had been gratified to note that Arnold Feely was maintaining a distinctly low profile, giving utterance only when it was strictly necessary in his client's interests. In fact, Feely's mind remained preoccupied throughout this period with matters beyond the confines of the court.

Operating also beyond the court's confines was Detective Chief Superintendent Samson, who was still trying to think of some way of penetrating the garage at number 18 Hall Mews without jeopardising his career. Though, to be honest, he had rather veered away from the notion that ex-Judge Whitby-Stansford was responsible for events at the Blackstone Club, mainly on account of the striking absence of any shared enthusiasm on the part either of his superior or his inferior officers. His enquiry seemed in danger of getting into the sort of doldrums that can so easily becalm a criminal investigation. One of his difficulties was that the original theft of the snuff-boxes and the return of the exploding one had no obvious common feature as criminal acts. The laboratory had now confirmed that the box sent to Mr Justice Pearn had, indeed, contained black powder (and not an explosive in the ordinary sense) which had been ignited by a clever but crude use of two non-safety matches as the lid was opened. The scientist who had examined it had added that it could have just as easily not gone off at all. Not that that seemed to make any difference, Samson reflected— other, of course, than to Mr Justice Pearn himself.

On the day that Brian was sent for trial, Roscoe threw

down the evening paper he'd been reading and said through a smothered yawn, 'Did you see this bit about Brian, Fiona?'

'What bit?' she asked quickly.

'It just says he's been committed for trial at the Old Bailey for murdering that old boy, that's all.'

'Poor love, he must think I've abandoned him,' she said with an air of tragedy.

'Isn't it about time you pulled yourself together?' Hive demanded impatiently. 'All you do is sit listlessly around like some ailing animal, which doesn't help anyone—not even Tanner.'

'It's your fault, you won't let me get in touch with him, what do you expect me to do?'

'Behave like an adult! Good grief, Fiona, *you* used to be the one who berated others when they put personal feelings before the cause.'

'I know. And that's the only reason I haven't been to see him.'

'Well, just bear up a bit longer,' Roscoe said, not unkindly. 'Hive's right.'

'I sometimes wonder if any one of us is right.'

'You don't mean that!'

'Why not? Isn't it a sign of strength to have doubts?'

'It may be if you overcome them, but not otherwise. You wouldn't have been one of us for so long if you really had doubts.'

'Anyway,' Hive broke in, 'you've only got to look about you for a couple of minutes to know we're right. We live in a sick, rotten and corrupt society perpetuated by the stinking self-interest of a few and the bovine indifference of the majority.'

'So what can we do about it?' Fiona asked suddenly.

Hive's eyes flashed. 'We can certainly do better than send silly practical jokes to Mr Justice bloody Pearn. I very much regret ever having permitted that folly. It's

174

achieved nothing other than to alert all the pigs in town.'
He paused and went on in the same angry tone, 'When
the proper time comes, we'll blow up the whole foully
reeking system, but, until then, let's not have any more
half-cock idiocies of that nature.'

'It was your idea that Brian should get that job at the
Blackstone Club,' Fiona said defiantly.

'In order to collect information about the top legal lack-
eys who infest the place when they're not exploiting the
working class in their courts. Not to go and get himself
involved in bourgeois thieving and arrested for murder.'

'You've no right to talk like that.'

'I have every right.'

'You'd never have known he had anything to do with
the theft of the snuff-boxes...'

'If he hadn't given one to you and you hadn't come
running here with it suggesting we should send it to Pearn
and the newspapers hadn't told the world it was one of
the stolen ones. No, if none of those things had happened,
I'd never have known.'

'There's no need to be sarcastic. You agreed it was a
good idea to send it to the pig judge.'

'That's right, you did, Hive,' Roscoe broke in. 'But all
this quarrelling isn't helping anyone, so what about both
of you belting up and listening to me?'

'Well, go on then,' Hive said testily.

'What we ought to be thinking about is how we can
help Gregor Maltby and his lot.'

'That's the whole bloody point, we can't! We shot our
bolt with that stupid snuff-box.'

'I wish you wouldn't go on about it as though you had
nothing to do with it! It was a joint decision.'

'I agreed against my better judgment.'

'But you agreed.'

'I thought Arthur was going to make a proper job of it
and fill it with explosive so, at least, it would have put

him out of action for the case, if not for ever.'

'Well, if we can't help Gregor, what are we going to do?'

'Helping Gregor Maltby was never the be all and end all of our existence. As far as I'm concerned, there've always been more important objectives.'

'Of course there are,' Roscoe said with a slight note of exasperation, 'but you have to make a start somewhere.'

'And a right paltry start we've made!'

'Christ! Here we go again!'

'The trouble with you, Roscoe, is that you've allowed your ideals to become contaminated by revisionism. So, of course, has Fiona to an even greater degree.'

Roscoe sighed heavily. 'I shall count slowly up to five hundred,' he said, 'and hope that by then we shall all be sufficiently cool to be able to discuss things without further recrimination.'

Fiona had scarcely listened to this last exchange between Hive and Roscoe. It had followed the now familiar pattern of Hive trying to assert his authority by a display of arrogance which all of them found increasingly irritating. But it had, at least, served one purpose, which was to give Fiona the determination to go to Brian's aid. She wasn't yet certain how she would set about it; only that she would and that none of them must learn of her intention.

CHAPTER TWENTY-THREE

As things turned out, Brian's trial came on more quickly than he'd expected. When he was told that the date was already fixed he wondered whether it had anything to do with the fact that he'd worked at the Blackstone Club. Perhaps the club felt that the cloud which hovered over him shut off a bit of sun from it as well.

In fact, however, the reason was more prosaic. In the first place Snaith & Co., being an efficient firm, had delivered briefs to counsel when a lot of firms would still only be in a preliminary stage of preparation, and, secondly, they had briefed Martin Ainsworth Q.C., with Paul Elson as his junior, and Ainsworth had said that, because of other trial commitments, he would be unable to do the case unless it came on quickly. The two Treasury Counsel briefed to appear on behalf of the prosecution had accepted the situation with the equanimity that characterised their attitude towards their work generally. If they weren't appearing in one court at the Old Bailey, they were appearing in another and it didn't make any odds in which order their cases were dealt with, provided they were given adequate notice.

On the day he was to appear at court, Brian dressed in a pair of newly-pressed oatmeal coloured slacks, a white shirt with deep mauve tie and a dark brown jacket. Rosa Epton had retrieved these from his room—that is, all apart from the shirt which was brand new. She had murmured something about the importance of looking neat and tidy, without appearing flashily dressed, and about a white shirt assisting to give the right impression. She had left Brian to speculate who had actually paid for the shirt. At all events, he was reasonably pleased with what he saw when he examined himself laboriously, square inch by square inch, in a small, scratched mirror. He was satisfied that he didn't look like a young man who went about murdering people. More like the office boy in a smart advertising agency, one of whom he'd once known.

About half an hour before his trial was due to start, Mr Snaith came down to the cell in which he'd been put on arrival at court, accompanied by the two counsel who were going to defend him. They were both wearing their wigs and gowns ready for court and shook hands with Brian when Snaith introduced them.

Brian stared at Ainsworth with the natural anxiety of one who feels he has delivered his fate into the hands of another. On the whole, he was reassured by what he saw, in particular by the warm blue eyes which gave him a friendly appearance. Elson, the junior counsel, was taller and broader and fat where his leader was thin. He had a round, shining face and the hands of a heavyweight boxer.

'I don't think we have anything to raise with you at this stage,' Ainsworth said. 'Mr Snaith has provided us with excellent instructions as to your defence and we'll do our best. Is there anything you want to ask me?'

Brian gulped. He had a sudden small boy's urge to blurt out the whole truth about his visit to Hersholt Street, to say he'd plead guilty to anything if only they'd forgo trying him for murder. He had nearly done so on a number of Rosa Epton's visits, but each time a voice had warned him that the truth at this stage was more likely than not to ensure his conviction for murder. His colours had been firmly nailed to the mast with the story he'd first given the police and there was no going back on it without increasing the peril of his situation. He realised that

his solicitor and counsel were all waiting for him to
speak. He swallowed hard.

'What's the name of the judge?' he asked, in a voice
which faltered.

'Mr Justice Osgood.'

'Is he all right?'

'You could do a lot worse.'

'Perhaps I know him.'

Ainsworth looked puzzled for a moment. 'Oh, you mean
through the Blackstone Club? No, he's not a member. Indeed, any judge who is would probably feel obliged to
disqualify himself from trying the case. By the same
token, neither of the prosecuting Counsel is a member of
the Blackstone. And nor am I or Mr Elson.' He smiled.
'Perhaps you hadn't realised there were so many members
of the legal profession who are not members of it.'

'How long will the case last, do you think, sir?'

'Three or four days. Not more than five.'

'When do I give evidence?'

'Certainly not today. Possibly not tomorrow. You can
never gauge what the tempo of a trial is going to be until
it has actually started. This judge is not a great speed
merchant.' Ainsworth put his hands up to his head, raised
his wig and resettled it. 'Perhaps there's one thing I ought
to mention, though I'm sure Mr Snaith has already. It's
the disappearance of your girl-friend, Miss Richey. She,
I imagine, would be able to support what you say about
the money—the five-pound notes—which the police found
in your room, being your savings. I think the prosecution
are bound to try and comment adversely on her absence
and though, of course, I'll seek to neutralise any criticism
they make, you ought to be warned what to expect.'

Brian nodded solemnly. Thank goodness he hadn't
named her as providing an alibi for the time he was
actually in Hersholt Street, but only for the night of the
theft of the snuff-boxes when he'd hidden at the club. And

try hard as they had the prosecution had been unable to find any legal excuse for introducing evidence of the Blackstone's burglary into the murder case, so Rosa had told him.

'Well, we'd better be getting up to court,' Ainsworth said.

A few minutes later, Brian was fetched from his cell and taken half-way up the flight of stairs which led into the rear of the dock. There he was motioned to wait while the senior of the two prison officers climbed the remaining stairs and peered about him as though from a submarine's conning tower.

Brian heard the judge make his entry, followed by the scuffing of feet as people sat down again. Then a voice called out, 'Put up Brian Tanner,' and he was given a prod by the officer behind him. A moment later he was standing in the front of the dock which seemed to occupy most of the floor space. It was one of the smaller of the old courts at the Old Bailey and Brian was almost embarrassed by the intimacy of his surroundings. He felt there was hardly anyone he couldn't touch just by stretching out. The judge was certainly uncomfortably close, though at this moment seemingly unaware of Brian's proximity as he busily re-arranged the items on his desk. Later Brian was to note that it didn't seem to matter how they were laid out, re-arranging them was always his first priority after taking his seat.

Brian glanced round the court looking for Rosa, but couldn't see her. Mr Snaith appeared to be on his own. Craning his head, he caught sight of Talbot, who quickly looked away. But otherwise there was no one he recognised.

The jury was sworn, nine men and three women, and Brian was formally delivered into their charge. From time to time one of them cast him a nervous glance as though he was a grenade which was about to go off.

Mr Justice Osgood nodded to senior prosecuting counsel to begin his opening address. Brian had the impression of someone uncoiling himself as counsel rose to his feet. He was not only well over six feet tall, but thin as a bean-pole. He had a lean face and his wig looked like an absurd piece of plumage on a rare bird. His manner could not have been in greater contrast with the last barrister who had prosecuted Brian and who had behaved like an eager terrier in a rat-infested farmyard.

Tenby, for that was his name, now began making the introductory observations which Brian recognised as stock from his previous time in court. As he addressed the jury, he bent slightly forward from the waist, resting his finger-tips delicately on the ledge in front of him.

He outlined the charge briefly and went on, 'Members of the jury, many cases are encumbered by points of law, but I make so bold as to say that this case has none. All it has is a simple issue of fact. Is this accused the person who murdered Harry Green? He says he is not. The prosecution say he is. At the end of the case you will have to decide on the evidence you have heard whether you're satisfied that the prosecution has proved his guilt.

'Let us now for a few minutes take a look at the evidence which the prosecution will be calling. Perhaps the most important witness—though by no means the only important one—is a Mr George Pratt, for he it was who saw the accused running away from the house where the murder was committed within what must have been minutes of Harry Green being battered to death. Mr Pratt was a casual passer-by, he didn't know the accused and had never seen him before. Nevertheless, he immediately picked him out on a subsequent identification parade. Cogent evidence, indeed, you may think, particularly when I tell you that the accused denies he was ever in Hersholt Street, or anywhere near it, on the evening in question.

'You may be wondering whether the accused and the deceased were known to each other. Well, they were, though it seems that the accused knew Green only as Stan, someone he had first met in a pub. On the accused's own admission, however, he had met Green, or Stan, some days before the murder and they had gone to a café just off Covent Garden for a cup of tea and a chat And then a few days later, not long before Green's death, they met again in the same place, the significance of which I will refer to in a moment...'

Brian switched his attention from prosecuting counsel to the jury, who appeared to be listening with rapt attention. He hoped they'd pay the same attention when his counsel's turn came.

'And now, members of the jury,' Mr Tenby was saying, 'let me tell you what happened when two police officers went to the room in Fulham occupied by the accused. With his permission they searched the room and, hidden behind a wall panel, they found a bag and in that bag they found seven hundred pounds in five-pound notes. Quite a lot of money you may think. Naturally, the accused was asked about it. And his explanation? It represented his savings.' Mr Tenby's voice had an almost sorrowful note that a better explanation had not been forthcoming. 'But the story doesn't end there, members of the jury, because the officers took possession of this bag of five-pound notes and you will hear that the fingerprints of the deceased were found on three of the notes.

'When later the accused is interviewed by Detective Chief Superintendent Chivers, he is again asked about his possession of the money and if he can account for Green's fingerprints being found on some of the notes The important point to note here, members of the jury, is that he wasn't told how many of the five-pound notes bore the deceased's fingerprints. Faced with this, the accused says that at his first meeting with Stan, alias Green, he lent him twenty-five pounds, and that at their second meeting Stan—or Green—repaid this sum with five five-pound notes. Why his fingerprints should have been on three of the notes, but not the other two, I don't know. But just pause for a moment and consider this—I hope I'm not being unfair—this remarkable relationship between the accused and the man he knew only as Stan.' Mr Tenby bent further forward to add emphasis to his words. 'They meet for the first time in a pub several months ago. They meet a second time quite by chance, it seems, and Stan borrows twenty-five pounds from the accused who conveniently has enough money on him to oblige. They meet a third time when Stan repays this short-term loan. Not long after this, Stan, or Green, is found murdered and his room ransacked so as to suggest that the murderer was looking for something. And then in the accused's possession is found this sum of seven hundred pounds. His savings, he tells the police...' Mr Tenby let his voice trail away as though it pained him to continue.

But continue he did while Brian's spirits sank lower and lower. He knew this was prosecuting counsel's opening speech, that it wasn't evidence and that the case lacked true perspective at this early stage. But for all that, it was almost more than he could bear to sit and listen to this persuasive reconstruction of his alleged crime with the deadly false inferences which Mr Tenby was inviting the jury to draw. And to make things worse, there were his twelve jurors hanging on to every word. Prosecuting counsel had them eating out of his hand and Brian could only sit impotently by. He squirmed on his chair as Mr Tenby went remorselessly on. All the explanations and excuses he had offered the police, which had sounded so good at the time, now had the appearance of paper banners after a boisterous demonstration. He turned his head and looked to where Talbot was sitting. The Blackstone's wine steward was leaning forward with his chin cupped in a hand and an expression of such satisfaction on his face that, for a second, Brian wondered whether he might not be the author of all his troubles. But how could he be! It was he, Brian, who had doped Talbot's nightcap, so how could Talbot have had anything to do with the burglary! Unless ... unless Brian had been duped even further than he realised and that the doping of Talbot was all part of a plan to show him as being in the clear. His glance passed on to someone standing just inside the door, whose expression seemed to betray more than a casual interest. Their eyes met and it was Brian who looked away discomfited by the other's stare.

Detective Sergeant Craddock had, in fact, been standing there since the case began. As he listened to counsel's opening, he had been observing the back of Brian's head. He had a theory that you could often gauge someone's reaction as well from rear observation as you could from studying their facial expression; in particular, someone under interrogation or in the dock of a criminal court. He could almost see Brian's confidence ebbing away as prosecuting counsel spoke, and well it might having regard to the strength of the case against him. Nevertheless, anyone with experience of criminal trials knew that witnesses could be frail, fallible creatures whose evidence didn't always match up to counsel's opening. And even when it did, it was a naïve person who didn't allow for the effect which cross-examination might have on it.

As Tenby concluded his opening and sat down, Craddock turned to leave the court.

'Hope to get my beans in this weekend,' whispered the uniformed officer on duty at the door as he held it open for Craddock. No matter what drama was taking place in his court, his talk to anyone he knew was always of gardening. Murderers, robbers and rapists might pass daily before his eyes, but it was peas, beans and dahlias which occupied his thoughts.

Craddock responded with a brief thumbs-up sign which could be interpreted any way the officer wished. As he was about to push through the outer door into the corridor he collided with Arnold Feely who was entering the court.

'Oh, hello,' Feely said without enthusiasm. 'What are you doing here?'

Craddock raised a quizzical eyebrow. 'The same as you, I imagine.'

'I've just slipped out of the Maltby trial for a few minutes.'

'Wanted to see how your club's ex-employee is faring, eh?'

'I'm interested, naturally.'

'Naturally! But I'm afraid you've missed Mr Tenby's opening speech.'

'Was it good?'

'Pretty effective, I thought. But I'm only an ignorant copper.'

Feely's mouth puckered as though he'd bitten on a lemon, but he made no comment, while Craddock watched him with a bantering expression. Giving his gown a tug up on to his shoulders, Feely passed into court. Craddock cast an eye over the waiting witnesses who were sitting there before making his way in search of a cup of coffee.

It was shortly before the luncheon adjournment that Tenby rose and said, 'Call George Pratt.'

So far the evidence had consisted of non-controversial matters and there was a flutter of interest as George Pratt came into court and, with a self-important air, thrust his way towards the witness-box. He took the oath in a ringing tone, adding a gratuitous 'So help me God!' at the end. Then he nodded civilly in the direction of the jury as though they were neighbours on the other side of a garden fence.

'Mr Pratt,' Tenby said in a voice to claim his attention. 'What is your full name, Mr Pratt?'

During the next quarter of an hour, he led Pratt painlessly through his evidence, which came out every bit as strong as it appeared on paper. And all the while Brian stared at the witness with an expression of impotent frustration.

As soon as prosecuting counsel sat down, his examination-in-chief concluded, the judge announced that the court would be adjourned until two o'clock and Brian was taken back to his cell.

'He wasn't a bad witness,' Elson said to Robin Snaith as they tidied their papers before leaving court. 'A bit too sure of himself, perhaps, but I think Martin's going to have his work cut out cracking him.'

Snaith nodded. 'I think Rosa's still confident he'll crack.' He glanced at his clerk who had arrived at court during the past half-hour. 'Aren't you?'

'Having heard him in the box, I'm more than ever sure he's lying.'

'We don't have to go as far as that. Merely, that he's mistaken.'

'He's more than mistaken.'

Elson shrugged. He knew Rosa Epton from other cases in which Snaith and Co. had briefed him and had considerable respect for her abilities. 'Let's hope the three women on the jury share your intuition,' he said with a smile. He moved towards the exit. 'Anyway, we'll see what the afternoon and Mr Ainsworth's cross-examination bring forth.'

Rosa found herself the last to leave the court and apologised to the officer on the door who was waiting to lock up.

'That's all right, miss,' he said genially, 'can't hurry a garden or the ladies is what I always say.'

She had just emerged into the corridor when someone

plucked at her sleeve. 'Excuse me but aren't you Brian's solicitor?'

Rosa turned her head to see who had spoken. For a second she was silent, then she said, 'Are you Miss Richey?'

'That's right. I'm his girl-friend. I've come to give evidence for him.'

'It's a pity you've left it so late,' Rosa observed and then relented when she saw the other girl wince.

'I couldn't get in touch with anyone before now. My own life was in a turmoil. Anyway, I'm sure Brian will have understood. It's not been easy for me.'

'It's not been easy for him either,' Rosa said sharply and immediately regretted having spoken when Fiona looked at her curiously. 'However, what is the evidence you want to give?'

'That he couldn't have done the murder because he was with me at the time.'

'With you?'

'Yes. So he couldn't have done it, could he?'

'But that doesn't agree with what he says. His evidence is to the effect that he was in the West End on his own at the material time. That's what he told the police!'

Fiona bit nervously at a knuckle. 'Are you sure?' she asked, with a look of wild despair on her face.

'Of course, I'm sure.'

'Yes, I'm sorry. I wasn't meaning to criticise you.' She brushed back a strand of hair which had fallen across her cheek. 'Everything's been so confused in my life recently. I suppose I must have been thinking of the other night.'

'What other night?'

'The night the club's snuff-boxes were stolen. Yes, I remember now, it was that night I was to say he was with me...' Her voice trailed away as she observed Rosa's expression. 'He has told you all about that, hasn't he?'

'I think,' Rosa said, after a pause, 'that we had better find a quiet corner where we can have a long talk.'

CHAPTER TWENTY-FOUR

Talbot had had difficulty in tearing himself away from the court, but determined to return in the afternoon if he could get through his work in time. He now had a new assistant at the club, so it should be possible.

He hadn't long returned from court when his new lad came into the wine pantry and said that someone in the smoking-room wanted a gin and tonic.

'Who?' Talbot demanded to know.

'I don't know his name,' the lad said in an offhand tone. 'The old geezer with bristles on the end of his nose.'

'Don't let me ever hear you speak of a member of the Blackstone in that manner again,' Talbot said severely.

'Well, how should I know his name? I've only been here a week. It's the old boy who always arrives early.'

'I know quite well who you mean. That's ex-Judge Whitby-Stansford.'

'O.K., well he wants a gin and tonic.'

'Are you sure? He always drinks pink gin.'

'I know it was something with gin.'

Talbot tut-tutted. 'Leave it to me. I'll serve him,' he said, reaching for the necessary bottles.

'The place is nothing but a lot of bloody old fossils,' the lad muttered beneath his breath as he wandered out of the wine pantry, 'and Talbot's the worst of them all!'

When Talbot reached the smoking-room, he found ex-Judge Whitby-Stansford on his own.

'Good morning, sir. It was your usual pink gin you wanted, I take it?'

'Actually, I asked for a gin and tonic. But that new boy of yours doesn't seem too bright. If you've brought a pink gin, I'll have that.'

'He didn't seem at all certain what you'd ordered, sir,' Talbot said shamelessly, 'and I took it upon myself to bring you your usual, but I can easily change it if you wish.'

'Don't bother, Talbot, I'll have what you've brought.'

'I've been to the Old Bailey this morning, sir,' Talbot said, after ex-Judge Whitby-Stansford had accepted his drink and paid for it. 'Young Tanner's trial started today.'

'You've not been very lucky with your assistants recently, have you? First him and now this moronic youth.'

'I'm afraid Tanner's a really wicked person. It's still my belief that he was behind the theft of the snuff-boxes.'

Ex-Judge Whitby-Stansford looked up over the top of his glass. 'As far as I can see,' he said, 'the police have completely bungled that enquiry. If Tanner or whatever his name is *was* concerned in the burglary they should have been able to find out by now. All they appear to be doing is thrashing about in the wildest manner and following up any hare-brain idea that enters their heads.'

'I never did like that Chief Superintendent Samson,' Talbot said, memories of his first interview with the officer still rankling. 'A terrible man with no idea how to behave.'

'Gave you a rough time did he?'

'He was so rude.'

'I didn't take to him, either.'

'You don't mean he had the impudence to treat you that way, sir?'

'I don't know what way we're talking about, Talbot. As far as I was concerned, he was just nosy and insinuating. Somebody had told him I was a collector and he obviously wondered if I mightn't have the snuff-boxes hidden away.'

'He didn't, sir!' Talbot exclaimed in a scandalised tone.

'I'd have much preferred he'd been straightforward and come along armed with a search warrant if that's what he suspected. I wouldn't even have minded his searching the garage where I store pieces I have no room for at home.' Ex-Judge Whitby-Stansford's face broke into a sabre-toothed tiger's smile. 'He wouldn't have found what he was looking for and I could have raised hell with his superiors afterwards.'

'Disgraceful conduct!' Talbot chimed in. 'And there's poor Sir John with a hand almost blown off on these very premises and the police don't do a thing!'

'Times are not what they were, Talbot.'

'Alas not, sir!'

'The good old virtues, which are still the desirable virtues, are held up to ridicule nowadays. Respect for authority and those exercising it has disappeared, replaced by a cheap cynicism.'

'I'm afraid that's so, sir.'

He drained his glass and held it out to Talbot. 'Bring me another, would you?'

'The same, sir?'

'Yes, I'd better stick to pink gin now. Perhaps you'd tell that new young man of yours to listen a little more carefully when he's taking an order.'

'I certainly shall, sir.'

Talbot hurried away, glancing at his watch. He wondered whether he should have a word with the secretary to see if he could be released from duty to enable him to get back to the Old Bailey for the afternoon session. It wasn't often he asked for favours and he didn't see why this one shouldn't be granted.

'Yes, all right, Talbot,' Colonel Tatham said.

'I'm very grateful, sir.'

'This new lad of yours will be all right on his own, will he?'

'Oh, very much so, sir. He's a most promising lad. I've been very favourably impressed by him.'

'Good! Well, I'll be interested to have a report on your return.'

Thus Talbot was squeezing back into the same seat he'd occupied in the morning as Mr Justice Osgood returned to the bench.

'Yes, Mr Ainsworth,' he said, peering at Brian's counsel over the top of his gold-rimmed half glasses. 'You wish to cross-examine the witness?'

'Yes, my lord, I do have a few questions to put to him,' Ainsworth said in a casual voice, while George Pratt listened to the exchange with an indulgent expression. He turned towards the witness. 'Tell me, Mr Pratt, how old are you?'

'I was forty-four last birthday, my lord,' Pratt replied, glancing round the court as if half-expecting a short burst of applause.

'I noticed that you put on a pair of spectacles to read the oath?'

'That's right, sir.'

'Can you read without spectacles, Mr Pratt?'

A crafty look came on George Pratt's face. 'If you're going to question me about my eyesight...'

'Don't anticipate my questions, Mr Pratt, just answer them as they come,' Ainsworth said pleasantly. 'Now, what's the answer to my last question?'

'Will you repeat it?'

'Yes. Can you read without spectacles?'

'Yes, I can.'

'Why did you put them on to read the oath?'

'It was sort of 'abit.'

'So you normally do wear them for reading?'

'I sometimes do, I sometimes don't.'

'The print on the oath card is quite large, wouldn't you say?'

'I don't recall.'

'Have a look at it again then.'

The usher stepped forward and held up the card with the words of the oath on it.

'Quite large print wouldn't you agree, Mr Pratt?'

'I suppose so.'

'Can you read it without your spectacles?'

'Naturally.'

'Go ahead, then.'

'I swear by ... by the ... the God...'

'Doesn't the word "almighty" appear before God?'

'Yes.'

'Difficult to read without your spectacles, is it?'

'It's just that you've made me nervous.'

'I don't want to make you nervous at all, I just want you to go on reading the words on the card without using your spectacles.'

Pratt glared at the card and held it first a bit closer to his face and then a bit further away.

'You've got me so nervous,' he said accusingly, 'that my eyes have gone all funny.'

'Very well, give the card back to the usher,' Ainsworth said in a tone of gentle reasonableness. 'Tell me this, Mr Pratt, how many pairs of spectacles do you own?'

'How do you mean?'

'I'd have thought it was a simple enough question,' the judge observed, putting down his pen and flexing the fingers of his writing hand.

'I just 'ave the one pair.'

'You don't have a different pair for watching television, for example?'

'Never watch it, do I! Lot of rubbish to my way of thinking.' He glanced once more round the court, encouraged by a faint ripple of titters.

'Well, even if you never watch television, Mr Pratt, do you wear spectacles for anything apart from reading?'

'No, why should I?'

'To enable you to see better,' Ainsworth said in a sweet tone.

'My sight's as good as yours!'

'From what you tell us, it's a good deal better than mine. But I'm here only to ask you questions, not to discuss our respective sight capabilities. I want now to come to the evening you've told the jury you were in Hersholt Street. You had, as I understand it, gone to meet a friend in a pub called the Plumbers Arms, but he never turned up. Is that right?'

'Yes. 'Cept he was more an acquaintance than a friend.'

'What was his name?'

'Paddy.'

'Just Paddy?'

'I didn't know 'is other name.'

'That makes it one all,' Elson whispered to Tenby behind Ainsworth's back. 'Our client's Stan against your witness's Paddy.'

Tenby grinned. Meanwhile Ainsworth went on, 'Have you seen Paddy since then?'

'No.'

'Tried to find him?'

''Ad no reason to.'

'I see. Anyway, after he failed to turn up at the Plumbers Arms that evening, you left and walked along Hersholt Street?'

'S'right.'

'And when you were about opposite number forty-two, you looked across and saw the accused dash out of the house and run off down the street?'

'S'right. 'Cept he paused before 'e runs off.'

'Looks across at you, does he?'

193

'Must 'ave done.'

'You had the definite impression that he saw you in the same way you saw him?'

'Yes.'

'No doubt about that?'

'No-o.' Pratt's tone indicated his suspicion of a trap.

'How long did he pause for?'

'Just a few seconds like.'

'One second? Two? Three? Or, say, ten? Seconds assume great importance on an issue such as this.'

Pratt gave a shrug as though he had no patience with such pettifogging questions.

'About three seconds.'

'And during that time you were staring at each other across the street?'

'It all 'appened in a flash.'

'No, Mr Pratt, it all happened in three seconds.'

''Ave it your own way!'

'It's your recollection the jury want to have.'

'You keeps on twisting what I say.'

'I'm trying to test, not twist, what you say. Anyway, to continue: what was it that caused you to look across the road in the first place?'

'I sort of 'eard a noise.'

'What sort of noise?'

'It must 'ave been your chap opening the door.'

'And?'

'I stopped and saw 'im like I've said.'

'And afterwards you went to the nearest telephone box and dialled nine, nine, nine?'

'S'right.'

'Why?'

'Why?' Pratt repeated, as though he found the world going mad.

'Yes, why?'

'Because of what I'd seen, of course.'

'All you'd seen was someone come out of a house and run off down the street. Why did that warrant an emergency phone call to the police?'

'Because he was acting so suspicious, that's why!'

'Do you phone the police every time you see someone come out of a house and dash down the street?'

''Course I don't!' Pratt said hotly.

'Ever done so before?'

'No.'

'Well, why on this occasion?'

'You could tell 'e'd been up to something from 'is expression. And I was right, anyway, wasn't I? 'E had.'

'Just keep calm, Mr Pratt,' the judge broke in. 'Counsel is only doing his duty.'

'So you were able to see his expression, were you?'

'Yes.'

'During these three seconds when you stared at one another across the street?'

'S'right.'

'What sort of an expression was it?'

'Kind of foxy.'

'I should have asked you this before, Mr Pratt, but I'm afraid I'd assumed your answer. Were you wearing your spectacles at the time?'

'I don't remember.'

'Don't remember!'

'No, I don't.' Pratt's tone was defiant.

'Is it likely you'd have been wearing them?'

''Ow do I know?'

'But I gathered you only wore them for reading and not always then. Isn't that what you told the jury?'

'I 'aven't told the jury anything. I'm only answering your twisting questions.'

'Behave yourself, Mr Pratt,' the judge said sharply. 'You do yourself less than justice when you give way to outbursts like that. Furthermore, everything said in the witness box is spoken for the benefit of the jury. It is they who are trying the issues, not counsel or myself. So just remember that.'

'I'm sorry, my lordship,' Pratt said in a chastened tone. 'But 'e keeps on at me so.'

'Would you like to sit down?'

'Thank you, your lordship.'

'And usher,' Mr Justice Osgood went on, 'give the witness a glass of water.'

Ainsworth leaned back and waited while George Pratt sipped the water with the air of an invalid.

'Shall I go on, Mr Pratt?' he enquired.

'That's up to you.'

'How often do you wear your reading spectacles when you're walking in the street?'

'Not often.'

'Ever?' There was no answer and Ainsworth continued, 'For example, did you wear them coming to court this morning?'

'No.'

'When do you last remember wearing them out in the street?'

'I don't remember.'

'So it's highly unlikely that you were wearing them that evening in Hersholt Street when it was dark anyway?'

'I suppose so. But there was a street light near the 'ouse 'e came out of.'

'Yes, I was coming to that. It's not a very well lit street, is it?'

'I've known worse.'

'And better?'

'Yes.'

'Am I right in saying that the lamp near number forty-two is one of those sodium ones that casts a yellow light?'

'S'right.'

'And makes people look a crude purple?'

'I was still able to see 'im properly and that's definite,' Pratt declared angrily.

Ainsworth stooped down to pick up something out of sight. When he straightened himself, he was holding up an enlarged photograph of about twelve inches by ten.

'Can you see what I'm holding in my hand, Mr Pratt?'

'It's a photograph.'

'That's quite right, but whose photograph is it? As you can see it's of a face, but whose face?'

Pratt leaned forward in the witness box peering at the blown up photograph which Ainsworth was now holding above his head. His eyes were screwed up, but suddenly he relaxed and a knowing look crept across his face.

'It's 'im,' he said triumphantly, pointing at Brian, 'I can see now.'

'As a matter of fact it's not,' Ainsworth remarked dryly. 'It's a full face photograph of this young lady sitting in front of me.'

And he indicated Rosa.

CHAPTER TWENTY-FIVE

As soon as the court had adjourned for the day and the judge had made his bows and departed, Tenby slid along counsel's row of seats to speak to Ainsworth.

'You appear to have been extremely well briefed on Mr Pratt's eyesight, if I may say so, Martin,' he said, with one eyebrow raised questioningly.

'Miss Epton, here, made a special study of it,' Ainsworth replied. 'The credit is hers.'

Tenby gave Rosa a thoughtful look. 'She made the bullets and all you had to do was fire them, eh! Nevertheless, I must commend you for your aim.' He paused. 'The point is, Martin, what do I say to the police?'

'About Pratt's evidence you mean?'

'Yes.'

'Well,' Ainsworth said slowly, 'I happen to know that Miss Epton, who has put a great deal of work into this case, is firmly of the opinion that Pratt is not merely mistaken in his identification, but has lied about it.'

'I imagine this afternoon's performance has reinforced her view. But that means there's been a frame-up.'

'Yes, but I don't have to go as far as suggesting that to the jury. Indeed, I'd sooner not do so. All I'm concerned with is their rejection of Pratt's evidence as reliable. I don't mind what conclusions they draw beyond that.'

'I can see that, but if, as now appears, Pratt is a deliberate perjurer, what ought the police to do? Wait till the trial is over or start making enquiries straightaway?'

'I don't know that it's for me to advise you on that, though I shan't criticise whichever course you take.'

'It's tricky,' Tenby murmured with a grimace. 'Anyway, thanks, Martin. I'd better have a word with Chivers before he goes. See you tomorrow morning.'

Robin Snaith and Rosa had listened to this exchange in silence. Then Ainsworth bid them good-night, leaving them to gather up their papers.

'I have something which I have to tell you,' Rosa said.

'Let's wait till we get back to the office.'

'It affects our client and we may need to see him before he's taken back to Brixton. It's rather important.'

When Rosa had finished speaking, Snaith said, 'You're right, we must go and put this to him at once.'

When they arrived in Brian's cell beneath the courtroom, they found him drinking a mug of tea. He beamed at them as they entered, being still buoyed up by the sense of euphoria engendered by the mangling his counsel had given Pratt.

'The jury can never convict me now, can they?' he exclaimed eagerly, jumping to his feet. 'And the police'll have to do Pratt for perjury, won't they?' His eyes sparkled. 'Wasn't Mr Ainsworth terrific? And you've both been terrific too.'

'It's not over yet,' Snaith remarked.

'But surely . . .'

'We've come to have a word with you,' Snaith interrupted, 'as a result of your girl-friend getting in touch with Miss Epton today.'

'Fiona, you mean?'

'Yes.'

Brian's glance went from one face to the other and his cheerful expression began to fade.

'What's up?' he asked anxiously. 'What's she told you?'

'She's told us that you were concerned in the theft of the snuff-boxes from the Blackstone Club and that you asked her to provide you with an alibi for that night. She has also told us that you did go to Green's address in Hersholt Street and that you found him dead when you got there. At least, that's what you subsequently told her.'

'It's the truth.' Brian's voice sounded as if his throat muscles had partially seized up.

'But it's *not* the evidence you were going to give in court.'

'I still didn't kill him, I swear I didn't.' He looked desperately from one to the other. 'Isn't Pratt's evidence proof that I've been framed?'

'Maybe it is, maybe it isn't. I'm not sure what I believe at the moment,' Snaith said. He did, in fact, now accept that Brian had been framed. It certainly accorded with what Rosa had thought all along. Nevertheless, he saw no reason why Brian shouldn't be made to sweat for a while. He now went on, 'But the position is that I can't be a party to putting forward a defence which I *know* to be untrue. And as you've now given me a version of your movements conflicting with that which has formed the basis of your defence up until this moment, I shall have to consider whether I oughtn't to withdraw from the case.'

'But need you tell Mr Ainsworth?' Brian said even more desperately.

'Are you now suggesting that I should deceive the counsel I've instructed to defend you?' Brian shook his head in a numbed sort of way. 'I'll think about this overnight,' Snaith said, 'and let you know in the morning what I've decided.'

Brian nodded miserably. He looked at Rosa for comfort but it seemed she deliberately avoided catching his eye. A few seconds later they had gone and he was once more alone in the cell. He sat down slowly and put his head in his hands, while black despair swept over him like flood water. Fate had given him one too many buffets. O.K., he was a fool; he was even a knave; but he wasn't a murderer. But who was going to believe that now?

Before leaving the Old Bailey, Robin Snaith put through a call to Martin Ainsworth's chambers. As a result, he and Rosa went straight round to Mulberry Court in the Temple without returning to their office.

'I'm sorry to come barging round at such short notice,' Snaith said, 'but I felt I had to let you know what's happened without delay.'

Ainsworth and Elson, who had come hurrying round to Ainsworth's chambers, listened to him in silence. When he had finished speaking, Ainsworth said thoughtfully:

'It fits, doesn't it?'

'Yes.'

'And it bears out what you've suspected all along, Miss Epton?' Rosa nodded. 'But it still leaves us to decide how to handle the situation,' Ainsworth continued. 'I obviously

can't put forward the evidence contained in the proof
you've sent me, now that I know it's not true. On the other
hand, if he gives evidence in accordance with what he now
says is the truth, he's in grave danger of being convicted,
Pratt's evidence notwithstanding. After all, to admit that
he lied to the police about his movements and that he
did in fact go to forty-two Hersholt Street that night is,
in the circumstances, tantamount to admitting to murder.' He stared for a minute out of the window with
frowning concentration. 'I think we are probably helped
by the fact Peter Tenby accepts that Pratt is a perjurer
and that our chap has been framed, presumably by whoever it was who arranged the Blackstone's burglary. If
he can persuade the Director and the police of this, I don't
see why we shouldn't obtain a short adjournment to
enable the police to go into action. Tomorrow's Friday;
supposing the judge adjourned the trial to Monday afternoon, that'd give them three and a half days to shake the
truth out of Pratt. It's not very long and we might later
have to ask for the jury to be discharged and a date set
for a fresh trial.' He smiled. 'Though I can't quite see
myself cross-examining Pratt a second time with such satisfactory results. But that's looking further ahead than
necessary. All we can do is to proceed one step at a time.
If you hang on, I'll phone Tenby now and put my suggestion to him.'

Obviously deciding that he'd prefer not to make such a
call in front of an audience, he left his room to telephone
from another.

When he returned about five minutes later, it was to say
that everything was arranged and that he and Tenby would
see the judge in his room before the court sat.

'I gather the police were pretty shaken by Pratt's performance and needed no persuasion. Needless to say, I
didn't tell Peter Tenby all you've told me. I just said
that as a result of Pratt's evidence something unforeseen

had cropped up on my side of the fence and that I thought an adjournment was the best way of getting ourselves sorted out.'

'Did he say whether the police had yet interviewed Pratt?'

'I gather they missed him at court. It seems he'd slipped away before they realised he'd gone.'

The next morning, a glum Detective Chief Superintendent Chivers reported to Tenby that George Pratt had vanished. He'd not returned to his address and no one had seen him since he'd left court the previous afternoon.

CHAPTER TWENTY-SIX

About twenty minutes to eleven the next morning, Arnold Feely whispered to one of the other counsel in the Maltby case that he was going to slip out of court for a few minutes. He rose and, giving Mr Justice Pearn a small bow, left.

When he arrived at the court next door, he was astonished to find it deserted. He espied Elson in the distance, however, and hurried after him.

'Osgood's adjourned the trial till Monday afternoon,' Elson said in answer to his question.

'Why's that?'

Elson lowered his voice. 'Between you and me and the gate-post, old boy, the case had begun to give off a strong smell of frame-up. A witness called Pratt, who gave evidence yesterday afternoon, lied from start to finish and we've adjourned for the matter to be looked into. That is, if the police can find Pratt, who's now done a bunk. Excuse me, old boy, I must dash . . .'

He hurried away, leaving Arnold Feely trying to re-assemble his thoughts which felt as if they'd been blown apart by the information he'd just received. It had even affected him physically so that he had to concentrate on the use of his legs in order to get back to his own court.

When he returned to his seat, he sank down in it and stared blankly at his open notebook. Slowly his mind seemed to come to life again. His first thought was one of relief that he was unlikely to be called on to utter a single word all day. A police officer had just begun to be cross-examined by Maltby who was clearly intent on spending most of that day exercising his forensic talents.

So it had happened at last! The moment he had pre-pared for and awaited, while still believing that it might never come and that events might still not catch up with him. Well, they had—or, rather, they would if he didn't move fast. And having laid his plans, it would be foolish to hesitate. What was the point of all his preparations, if he was going to lack resolution when the moment for decision came. His decision had been made weeks before, it was only the timing of its execution which had re-mained uncertain. But no longer!

When the court adjourned at lunchtime, he told one of his fellow defending barristers that he was feeling ill and was going home to bed. Etiquette really required that he should also let the judge know, normally through his clerk, but to hell with etiquette! Etiquette called on you to knock on a strange door before entering, but you didn't stop to do so if your intention was to lob a live grenade into the room.

And what Arnold Feely was about to do was to blow up his life as it had been up till this moment . . .

By mid-afternoon he was on a plane to Paris and the

next day he'd be in South America. With a numbered Swiss bank account, which he had been feeding for over a year, to support him, he had no immediate worries.

As the plane crossed the coast and headed out over the Channel, he looked down on what he thought would probably be his last ever view of England, and found himself unmoved.

He tried to imagine Marcia's reaction when she discovered he'd gone. There'd certainly be surprise, probably anger and possibly panic. He hoped there'd be panic. She deserved to suffer after the way she had treated him. If it hadn't been for her, none of this would ever have happened.

He accepted another glass of champagne from the smiling stewardess and tried to think of the various things he'd left undone in his hasty departure. They'd go through all his papers, of course, and in his desk in chambers, they'd find the letter hinting at Marcia's infidelity. Well, he'd sent it to himself meaning that it should be brought to light one day, though he hadn't then envisaged the present circumstances. At the time, it had seemed a good idea to have it up his sleeve ready to flourish at anyone probing into his wife's extra-mural activities. Now, it would be found and they could make what they liked of it.

He thought of the Blackstone Club. That was somewhere he wouldn't miss. He'd so often been made to feel he didn't quite belong. His qualifications might be impeccable, but his breeding was not. Some could override such a deficiency, but he'd always been aware of his inability to do so. It showed and moreover he lacked those compensatory facets that could enable a dustman and a nobleman to talk on equal terms.

And no one had been able to make him feel more notbelonging than that arch old snob, Talbot.

He wondered what would happen now to Brian. A likeable young rogue in some ways. He was probably destined to spend his life in and out of prison. He certainly wouldn't always have the luck to be acquitted.

Feely had always had a good memory for faces and that was how he had come to recognise Brian the first time he saw him working in the Blackstone. The face was immediately familiar and then he recalled how he had happened to enter the court where Brian was being tried on a previous occasion and had stopped for ten minutes or so while he was giving evidence. And a zestful performance it had been, too!

The plane was making its descent to land at Orly.

Feely checked his travel documents before closing his briefcase. Then he fastened his seat-belt and gazed out at house-tops below. In the distance he could see the Eiffel Tower.

The time for reflecting on the past was over. Now it was only the future which mattered.

CHAPTER TWENTY-SEVEN

At about the time that Feely's plane was over the English Channel, Detective Inspector Pendleton plucked from his in-tray the radio-ed message which had recently landed there.

It was addressed to all stations in the Metropolitan Police District and asked for immediate notification of the whereabouts of one George Pratt who had disappeared the previous day after giving evidence at the Old Bailey. A description of Pratt with his last known address was provided.

Pendleton frowned. The name seemed to ring a bell ... someone had mentioned it to him in connection with a case and then he'd heard no more ... The nagging at the back of his mind increased the frown on his face ... He was sure he'd expected to hear more.

He read the message a second time. Perhaps this was the same case, and yet that didn't seem to fit in with his hazy recollection.

In the end, he decided to go and find out. He went along to the C.I.D. general office, but a search there led him nowhere. He entered the next-door room, neither of whose two occupants were in, and rummaged amongst the dockets that lay out on their desks. He also flipped through those in a green filing cabinet. But he found nothing relating to George Pratt.

Puzzled, and at the same time irked by his own memory failure, he began opening the drawers of one of the desks. They revealed nothing save its user's personal odds and ends. He now turned his attention to the second desk. The first three drawers left his now insistent curiosity unsatisfied. The fourth drawer was locked.

It was against his instructions to lock any working papers in a desk drawer. That was what the filing cabinet was for. It was secure and others could get at the contents if need be.

He pulled out his own bunch of keys. It was just possible that one of them might fit. The second key he tried almost did and he was jiggling it hopefully when he heard someone behind him. Glancing round, he found Detective Sergeant Craddock staring at him with an expression of blazing anger.

'What the hell are you doing?' he demanded.

'I want this drawer opened immediately,' Pendleton replied.

'You've no right to go prying in my desk like that. If I reported this, you'd be disciplined.'

Pendleton counted slowly up to five before trusting himself to speak again.

'If you don't open this drawer at once, I shall have you suspended from duty.'

A small vein began to throb visibly in Craddock's temple.

'Why should I open it? It's only private things.'

'Prove it to me.'

'You haven't said why.'

'I want to be satisfied there are no official papers in there.'

Craddock who had taken a step towards the desk paused like an animal scenting fresh danger in the wind.

'What papers?'

'Relating to someone called George Pratt.' Craddock's head shot up and Pendleton went on, 'It was you, wasn't it, who mentioned Pratt to me some weeks ago? I remember now, you had a few more enquiries to make but thought you'd have enough to charge him with handling stolen property. Antique silver, wasn't it? You've not referred to the case since . . .'

'There never was enough evidence.'

'Where's the docket?'

'With registry, I suppose.'

'It's not.'

'I can't help then.'

'You can—and will—by opening that drawer.'

'I'm going.'

'Leave this room without unlocking that drawer and you'll find yourself in a cell.'

Slowly, and with every muscle demonstrating rebellion, Craddock produced a bunch of keys from his trouser pocket and unlocked the drawer.

Pendleton bent down and pulled it sharply open. It was crammed with a miscellany of items which his determined fingers scattered aside. At the bottom, underneath

207

everything else, was a buff-coloured paper folder. On its outside was inscribed the name George Pratt.

Impatiently, Pendleton flicked it open. It contained working notes and some manuscript statements, amongst them one signed 'G. Pratt'. A quick glance was sufficient to see that it amounted to a confession of handling a stolen George III silver coffee pot.

'Well?' Pendleton said, looking up. But the room was empty.

He dashed to the door and then downstairs to the front of the station.

'Have you seen Sergeant Craddock?' he asked the uniformed officer on duty.

'No, sir. Shall I see if I can find him for you?'

But Pendleton had dashed off again before the officer had finished speaking. He tore out into the yard at the rear, just as two young P.C.s were getting out of a panda car.

'Either of you seen Sergeant Craddock?'

'Yes, sir. He was driving off as we came in. He looked as if he was in a bit of a hurry.'

Pendleton nodded his thanks and hurried back into the station.

A few minutes later, he was speaking to Detective Chief Superintendent Chivers and within half an hour an order had gone forth that Detective Sergeant Craddock was to be detained on suspicion of having attempted to defeat the course of justice.

It took a bright young Detective Sergeant, just back from Detective Training School, to point out, however, that this was not an arrestable offence without a warrant. He was hoping to have the opportunity of expounding on the section of the relevant Act of Parliament, as interpreted by various judicial decisions, when Pendleton cut him short.

'Then we'll get an immediate warrant,' he snarled. 'And

if he slips out of the country through some legal loophole, I'll be breakfasting off Detective Sergeants for the next twelve months.'

CHAPTER TWENTY-EIGHT

When every officer in the Metropolitan Police is on the look-out for somebody, that somebody stands a good chance of being spotted once he wanders abroad. If, of course, he remains under cover, then the chances dwindle to vanishing point.

Though George Pratt had been told to lie low for a while, he didn't interpret this as meaning he shouldn't go out at all; certainly not that he stay away from public houses. If ever a man had, in his own view, earned a few pints of beer, it was George Pratt. Moreover, though Craddock had threatened him with dire consequences if he didn't obey the instruction, Pratt never dreamt that every copper in London had an eye open for him.

He had moved into a modest room in a seedy residential area of North London, paid for by Craddock. The landlady knew him simply as Mr West.

About seven o'clock on this same Friday, he set off for a drink. The pub was some distance away and he remained there until it closed. When he left, he was feeling benevolent for the first time since his abrasive experience in the witness box on the previous day.

It was while he was waiting at a bus stop on his way home that a young constable, who had obviously been watching him without his being aware of the fact, approached.

'Excuse me, but is your name George Pratt?'

Pratt jumped visibly. ''Course it ain't,' he said with a slight belch.

'What is it then?'

'What, my name?'

'Yes.'

'It's ... it's ... it's Smith.'

'John Smith, I expect,' the constable said with a grim little smile.

'S'right.'

'Do you have any documents on you to prove who you are?'

Pratt produced a battered-looking wallet and made a pretence at looking through it.

'No, nothing 'ere.'

'May I look?'

'And nick my money? Not likely!'

'Then I must ask you to come along to the station. I'm sure we'll be able to sort this out quite quickly.'

'I won't come.'

The constable took a deep breath. 'You don't want me to arrest you, do you?'

It was at that point Pratt gave the constable a vigorous push and tried to jump on a bus which was just pulling away. It wasn't a very sensible action as the constable, who was young and athletic, simply grabbed him and said with obvious relief, 'That was an assault. Now, I am arresting you.'

Within an hour of Pratt's arrival at the police station, Detective Chief Superintendent Chivers was there.

'Now then, George,' Chivers said, when they were seated in one of the C.I.D. rooms, 'you and I have got a lot to talk about. What happens after that depends entirely on you.'

'What d'you mean?'

'Tell me the truth and I'll do what I can to help you.

Though I can't give any promises, mind you; you'll just
have to trust me on that. But string me along with the
sort of lies you told in court yesterday and I'll throw the
whole charge book at you.' He paused and gave Pratt a
thoughtful look. 'It may help to unknot your tongue if I
tell you there's a warrant out for Sergeant Craddock's
arrest.'

'Is that the truth?'

'Yes.'

'Cor!'

'He was on your tail over that stolen silver coffee pot,
wasn't he? He got a confession of handling out of you.'

'Because he threatened me.'

'I suspect the threats came afterwards. If you helped
him, he'd see you weren't charged. Correct?'

'I didn't mean no harm.'

'What was it he wanted you to do?'

'Just be in 'Ersholt Street near number forty-two and
wait for that young chap to run away.'

'And then?'

'Phone the police and 'ang around to tell 'em what I'd
seen.' With a touch of spirit, he added, 'There was nothing
wrong in that. I only told what I'd seen with my own
eyes.'

'Your own eyes!' Chivers said derisively. 'You couldn't
tell a man in a space suit bobbing at the end of your
nose, so don't try that lark. I suppose Craddock showed
you a photograph of Tanner before you attended the
identification parade?' Pratt nodded. 'And you knew quite
well that Green had been murdered by Craddock?'

'No, I swear I didn't. All he told me was this young
chap would be going to the 'ouse and I was to 'ang around
until he run out and then raise the alarm.'

'Of course you knew what had happened inside! Otherwise, why were you to wait for Tanner to *run* out or *dash*
out?'

Pratt squirmed. 'He only sort of 'inted. I didn't actually know.'

'You knew that Tanner was to be lured to the house where he'd find a dead body and you were there to alert the police as soon as he fled from the scene. That was the plan, wasn't it?'

'He never said anything about luring the young chap.'

'Come off it, George. You knew quite well what was going to happen, didn't you? What's more you fell in with the idea.'

'I 'ad to or 'e'd 'ave 'ad me in the nick. And I've 'ad enough.'

'You were the willing party to a deliberate frame-up, weren't you?' Chivers went on remorselessly.

'Not willing. Honest, I wasn't. 'E's an evil man, that Sergeant Craddock. 'Asn't an ounce of mercy in 'im.'

'I don't know as you have very much. You were quite ready to perjure away an innocent man's liberty.'

' 'E's not innocent.'

'He's innocent of Green's murder. Did Craddock tell you why he killed Green?'

' 'E was behaving a bit troublesome about 'is cut.'

'His cut over the theft of the snuff-boxes?'

'Yes.'

'So by murdering Green and framing Tanner for it, Craddock was effectively drawing up the ladder which linked himself with the crime,' Chivers observed in a thoughtful tone. 'When did you last see Craddock?'

'Last night.'

'Any idea where he might be now?'

'No. If I 'ad, I'd tell you straight. 'E's got me into enough trouble.'

'And himself as well!'

CHAPTER TWENTY-NINE

Marcia Feely gave a friendly smile to the police officer on duty who waved her Dormobile through the dock gate. She joined the queue of cars waiting to pass into the Customs shed.

Loading had already begun and the line of vehicles moved slowly forward. She knew from previous experience that once through the farther gate she'd be directed to one of the Customs bays where formalities were always quickly completed. It was on return journeys that you were liable to be held up while a car ahead was searched from stem to stern.

She glanced down at the empty passenger seat beside her to make sure she had all the necessary documents ready for examination.

A few minutes later, she had passed into the shed and was directed to the bay on the far left. The two cars in front of her were soon dealt with and she drew up beside the waiting Customs official, handing him her documents with a sunny smile.

'Travelling alone, madam?'

'Yes. I'm meeting my husband in Paris and we're motoring on to Italy for a holiday. He had some business to attend to and flew over ahead of me.'

The official's only reaction to this information was to bend down and peer beneath the Dormobile.

When he straightened up again, he said, 'Would you mind getting out for a moment, madam?'

Marcia Feely frowned. 'What for?'

'Just routine, madam.'

He wasn't going to tell her they had received a reliable tip-off that a consignment of drugs might be smuggled out that day or the next in a van-type of vehicle and that Customs were searching everything that came broadly within that category.

'Oh, really!' she said in an exasperated voice. 'Why do you have to pick on an unfortunate woman travelling alone?' She glanced impatiently at her watch.

'It's all right, madam, the boat won't sail without you.' As he spoke, he opened the driver's door and stood aside to let her get out.

With a grim expression, she stood and watched him examine the floor of the cab of the vehicle. Her frustration was increased by the realisation that cars at other bays were flowing freely with the minimum of hold-up.

The official withdrew from the cab and stood up.

'Finished?' she asked querulously.

'Just unlock the back, would you please, madam?'

'Oh, surely not! This is too ridiculous! Why am I being victimised like this?'

She stamped her foot angrily, while the Customs official just stared at her with maddening patience.

'If you turn things upside down in there and make a mess, I shall make an official complaint to the head of your department,' she said furiously, opening the rear of the Dormobile.

The official stepped inside and began a methodical examination of the interior, while Marcia Feely paced up and down outside in what was now obvious agitation, which confirmed him in his belief that she had something to hide.

It was not drugs, however, that he found in the locker beneath one of the bunk beds, but, crouched in a foetal position, Detective Sergeant Craddock.

CHAPTER THIRTY

At two o'clock sharp on the Monday afternoon, Tenby rose to his feet on cue from the judge.

'My lord, since this case was adjourned last Friday, various urgent enquiries have been made as a result of which another person has now been detained in connection with the murder of Harry Green, and will, I understand, shortly be charged with that offence. I have had an opportunity of discussing this new development with the police and those instructing me and we are all satisfied that the proper course is for the Crown to offer no further evidence against this accused and to ask for him to be discharged. Your lordship will appreciate that it is not in the public interest I should say more at this stage.'

Tenby sat down and Mr Justice Osgood glanced towards Martin Ainsworth who rose to his feet.

'My lord, I also appreciate the reasons for saying little on this occasion and all I wish to do in open court is stress the fact that my client has all along denied any responsibility for Green's death and that the Crown, by adopting their present course, now clearly accept what he has always maintained.'

Mr Justice Osgood nodded and turned towards the jury. 'Members of the jury, you have heard what prosecuting counsel has just said. As the accused has been committed to your charge, it is for you now, on my direction, to return a formal verdict of not guilty. Will you kindly do so...'

A moment later, Brian had been acquitted in an atmosphere as devoid of emotion as that of a second-hand shoe shop. Surely someone in court might have smiled at him. He was sure Rosa would have done, but he'd been unable to spot her.

He was hardly back in the cell area, where he was taken to pick up his belongings, when Mr Snaith appeared.

Brian shook him warmly by the hand. 'Thank you very much, sir, for all you've done for me.'

Snaith, who was used to not being thanked by acquitted clients (many of whom appeared to feel that as the State had paid for their defence, the State could do any thanking that was called for), smiled and said, 'I'll pass your thanks on to Rosa. She did all the hard work on your defence.'

'I was hoping to see her this afternoon . . .'

'She had to go to another court,' Snaith said firmly. In a different tone he went on, 'I'd better explain what's happened as I expect you're a bit mystified. I didn't have time before court to give you more than bare details. As I told you, a Detective Sergeant Craddock is going to be charged with Green's murder. It was he who set up the burglary at the Blackstone.'

'But I've never even heard of him. How did he get on to me?'

'Through Feely, who recognised you from having seen you in court before. Craddock was friendly with the Feelys, in particular Mrs Feely. It seems that her shop had become a front for disposing of stolen antiques and that Craddock used his contacts in the criminal world to keep her supplied.'

'What about Mr Feely?'

'From all accounts, he was the reluctant third of the trio. Anyway, he's now fled the country.'

Brian was thoughtful for a moment. 'Is everything over as far as I'm concerned?'

'You'll probably be called as a witness against Craddock and Mrs Feely.'

'Mrs Feely? Is she being charged, too?'

'In connection with the stolen snuff-boxes.'

Brian looked doubtful. 'I don't know as I want to give evidence.'

'If you don't, the police might be tempted to charge you with your part in the burglary.'

'I see! So I better had.'

'It's generally sensible to recognise whose is the whip hand.' Brian nodded slowly and after a pause Snaith went on, 'Incidentally, Miss Richey is waiting to see you outside.' He fixed Brian with a hard stare. 'Just before we part, I should like to give you a word of advice. I don't often offer advice to my acquitted clients because it's generally a waste of breath, but I hope you may heed what I say.'

'I shall.'

'You'd better hear what I've got to say first. It's this: you've now had three acquittals. It's a record you can't possibly hope to keep up, so the only alternative is to steer clear of the courts—or, rather, of the crime that leads people into them.' He smiled. 'It's all right to appear as a prosecution witness!' Holding out his hand, he said, 'Good-bye and good luck.'

When Brian emerged into the public corridor, Fiona, who had obviously been told just where to wait for him, threw herself into his arms.

'Oh, love,' she said with a half-sob, half-gasp. 'Oh, it's so wonderful to feel you again.' They kissed, passionately on her part and with growing fervour on his. Eventually, she disengaged her head and gazed at him like a starving person surveying a banquet. She took his hand. 'Mr Snaith has shown me a way to get out of the building, avoiding the press.'

Brian allowed himself to be led. At the moment, he

was just grateful to be free and was ready to let others decide events for him—until the next day, at any rate.

'Where are we going?' he asked.

'I've taken another room. It's in Bayswater.'

'Nearer to your lot?'

She shook her head vigorously. 'I've finished with them. We had a flaming row and all split up. Roscoe's gone to Germany and Hive's got in with another group.'

'Did the police never get on to them over that snuff-box?'

She shook her head. 'And you won't say anything, will you?'

Mr Snaith's parting words to him still rang in his head. 'Don't tell me anything and then I can't say anything.'

She gave his hand an affectionate squeeze. 'Let's forget the past and only look to the future.'

Brian was all for that, though he was far less certain than Fiona appeared to be that their future lay together. However, he would enjoy her company for the next few days and then see how he felt.

On reflection, it might be better to stay with her until everything was finally resolved—and heaven alone knew what his feelings about *anything* would be by then.

>>> If you've enjoyed this book and would like to discover more great vintage crime and thriller titles, as well as the most exciting crime and thriller authors writing today, visit: >>>

The Murder Room
Where Criminal Minds Meet

themurderroom.com

www.ingramcontent.com/pod-product-compliance
Ingram Content Group UK Ltd.
Pitfield, Milton Keynes, MK11 3LW, UK
UKHW040435280225
455666UK00003B/77